English Girl in New York

Scarlet Wilson

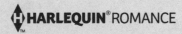

ISBN-13: 978-0-373-74274-5

ENGLISH GIRL IN NEW YORK

First North American Publication 2014

Copyright © 2014 by Scarlet Wilson

Printed in U.S.A.

www.Harlequin.com

"I told you—I'm not an expert in all this. I have no idea how to look after a baby!"

Dan reached over and touched her hand. She was getting flustered again, starting to get upset. "Carrie McKenzie?" He kept his voice low.

"What?" she snapped at him.

Yep, he was right. Her eyes had a waterlogged sheen. She was just about to start crying.

He gave her hand a little squeeze. "I think you're doing a great job."

Those dark brown eyes were still looking at her.

Still looking as if he understood a whole lot more than he was letting on. As if he'd noticed the fact she was seconds away from cracking and bursting into floods of tears.

But he couldn't, could he? Because he didn't really know her at all.

Daniel Cooper was all-action New York cop. The kind of guy from a romance movie, who steals the heroine's heart and rides off into the sunset with her. A good guy.

The kind of guy who looks after an abandoned baby.

She was trying to swallow, but her mouth was drier than a desert.

She looked down to where his hand covered hers. It was nice. It felt nice.

And that was the thing that scared her most.

When was the last time someone had touched her like that? At the funeral? There had been a lot of hand squeezing then. Comfort. Reassurance. Pity.

Not the same as this.

He smiled at her. A sexy kind of smile. The kind that could take her mind off the nightmare she was currently in.

Dear Reader,

I'm really delighted that this is my tenth book for Harlequin® and my first for the Harlequin Romance line.

This book is set in New York—a place where I celebrated my fortieth birthday with my family. It is a fantastic city. The Waldorf Astoria was a dream to stay in, and we loved visiting the American Museum of Natural History and walking back across Central Park.

In my story, Central Park is closed because of the huge deluge of snow. This actually happened when my friend stayed in New York a few years ago and is based on fact—not fiction!

Carrie, my lonely Londoner, and Dan, my hunky New York cop, find themselves snowed in at home in West Village. They barely know each other, but when an abandoned baby turns up on their snow-covered doorstep, it's definitely time for the temperature to rise a few notches!

I hope you enjoy my first story for the Harlequin Romance series.

Please feel free to visit me and tell me what you think, at www.scarlet-wilson.com.

Happy reading!

Scarlet

Scarlet Wilson wrote her first story at age eight and has never stopped. Her family has fond memories of *Shirley and the Magic Purse,* with its army of mice, all with names beginning with the letter *M.* An avid reader, Scarlet started with every Enid Blyton book, moved on to the Chalet School series and many years later found Harlequin®.

She trained and worked as a nurse and health visitor, and currently works in public health. For her, finding medical romances was a match made in heaven. She is delighted to find herself among the authors she has read for many years.

Scarlet lives on the West Coast of Scotland with her fiancé and their two sons.

This is Scarlet Wilson's debut novel for Harlequin Romance. Other titles by the author are available in ebook format from www.Harlequin.com.

My first Harlequin Romance story has to be dedicated to my own three personal heroes—Kevin, Elliott and Rhys Bain. This story is set in New York, and they helped me celebrate my fortieth in New York in style!

Also to my editor Carly Byrne, who is soon to have her own adventure! Thank you for your support and I hope to collaborate with you on lots more stories x

CHAPTER ONE

THE SUBWAY RATTLED into the station, the doors opened and Carrie felt herself swept along with the huddled masses on the platform, barely even looking up from her hunched position in her woefully thin coat. It had looked better on the internet. Really. It had.

She resisted the temptation to snuggle into the body in front of her as the carriage packed even tighter than normal. Just about every train in the city had ground to a halt after the quick deluge of snow.

The streets had gone from tired, grey and bustling to a complete white-out with only vaguely recognisable shapes in a matter of hours.

An unprecedented freak snowstorm, they were calling it.

In October.

In the middle of New York.

The news reporters were having a field day—

well, only the ones lucky enough to be in the studio. The ones out in the field? Not so much.

And Carrie appreciated why. Her winter coat wasn't due to be delivered for another two weeks. She could die before then. Her fingers had lost all colour and sensation ten minutes ago. Thank goodness she didn't have a dripping nose because at these temperatures it would freeze midway.

'They've stopped some of the buses,' muttered the woman next to her. 'I'm going to have to make about three changes to get home tonight.'

An involuntary shiver stole down her spine. *Please let the train get to the end of the line.* This part of the subway didn't stay underground the whole way; parts of it emerged into the elements and she could already see the thick white flakes of snow landing around them.

A year in New York had sounded great at the time. Magical even.

A chance to get away from her own *annus horribilis*.

A chance to escape everyone she knew, her history and her demons.

The only thing she'd taken with her was her exemplary work record.

In the black fog that had been last year it had been her one consistently bright shining star.

She should have known as soon as her boss had invited her into his office and asked her to sit down, giving her that half sympathetic, half cut-throat look. He'd cleared his throat. 'Carrie, we need someone to go to New York and represent the London office, leading on the project team for the next year. I understand this year has been difficult for you. But you were my first thought for the job. Of course, if it feels like too much—or the timing is wrong…' His voice had tailed off. The implication was clear. There were already two interns snapping at her heels, anxious to trample her on the way past.

She'd bit her lip. 'No. The timing is perfect. A new place will be just what I need. A new challenge. A chance for some time away.'

He'd nodded and extended his hand towards her. 'Congratulations. Don't worry about a thing. The firm has an apartment in Greenwich Village in the borough of Manhattan. It's a nice, safe area—easily commutable. You'll like it there.'

She'd nodded numbly, trying not to run her tongue along her suddenly dry lips. 'How long until I have to go?'

He'd cleared his throat, as if a little tickle had appeared. 'Three weeks.' The words were followed by a hasty smile. 'One of the partners will be leaving for business in Japan. He needs to brief you before he leaves.'

She'd tried hard not to let the horror of the time frame appear on her face as she'd stood up and straightened her skirt. 'Three weeks will be fine. Perfectly manageable.' Her voice had wavered and she'd hoped he didn't notice.

He'd stood up quickly. 'Perfect, Carrie. I'm sure you'll do a wonderful job for us.'

The train pulled into another station and Carrie felt the shuffle of bodies around her as the passengers edged even closer together to let the hordes of people on the platform board. It seemed as if the whole of New York City had been sent home early.

A cold hand brushed against hers and a woman gave her a tired smile. 'They've closed Central Park—one of the trees collapsed under the weight of the snow. I've never heard of that before.' She rolled her eyes. 'I'm just praying the school buses get home. Some of the roads are closed because they don't have enough snow ploughs and the grit wasn't due to be delivered for another two weeks.' Her face was flushed as she continued to talk. 'I've never seen it so bad, have you? I bet we're all snowed in for the next few days.'

Carrie gave a rueful shrug of her shoulders.

'I'm not from around here. I'm from London. This is my first time in New York.'

The woman gave a little sigh. 'Poor you. Well, welcome to the madhouse.'

Carrie watched as the train pulled out of the station. It didn't seem to pick up speed at all, just crawled along slowly. Was there snow on the tracks, or was it the weight of too many passengers, desperate to get home before the transport system shut down completely? *Please, just two more stops.* Then she would be home.

Home. Was it home?

The apartment in West Village was gorgeous. Not quite a penthouse, but part of a brownstone and well out of her budget. West Village was perfect. It was like some tucked away part of London, full of gorgeous shops, coffee houses and restaurants. But it still wasn't home.

Today, in the midst of this snowstorm, she wanted to go home to the smell of soup bubbling on the stove. She wanted to go home to the sound of a bubble bath being run, with candles lit around the edges. She wanted to go home somewhere with the curtains pulled, a fire flickering and a warm glow.

Anything other than her own footsteps echoing across the wooden floor in the empty apartment, and knowing that the next time she'd talk to another human being it would be with the man who ran the coffee stall across the street on the way to work the next morning.

She wrinkled her nose. It might not even come to that. The sky was darkening quickly. Maybe the woman next to her was right. Maybe they would end up snowed in. She might not speak to another human being for days.

She shifted the bag containing the laptop in her hands. She had enough work to last for days. The boss had been clear. Take enough to keep busy—don't worry about getting into the office. If the snow continued she couldn't count on seeing any of her workmates.

The people in her apartment block nodded on the way past, but there had never been a conversation. Never a friendly greeting. Maybe they were just used to the apartment being used by business people, staying for a few weeks and then leaving again. It would hardly seem worthwhile to reach out and make friends.

A shiver crept down her spine and her mind started to race.

Did she have emergency supplies? Were there any already in the apartment? How would she feel being snowed in in New York, where it felt as if she didn't know a single person?

Sure, she had met people at work over the past two months. She'd even been out for a few after-work drinks. But the office she worked in wasn't a friendly, sociable place. It was a fast-paced, frenetic, meet-the-deadline-before-you-die kind of place. She had colleagues, but she wasn't too sure she had friends.

The train shuddered to a halt at Fourteenth Street and the door opened. 'Everybody out!'

Her head jerked up and the carriage collectively groaned.

'What?'

'No way!'

'What's happening?'

A guard was next to the door. 'This is the last stop, folks. Snow on the tracks. All trains are stopping. Everybody out.'

Carrie glanced at the sign. Fourteenth Street. One subway stop away from the apartment. She glanced down at her red suede ankle boots. She could kiss these babies goodbye. The ground outside was covered in thick, mucky slush. She didn't even want to think about what they'd look like by the time she reached the apartment.

The crowd spilled out onto the platform and up towards the mezzanine level of the station on Fourteenth Street. Carrie could hear panicked voices all around her trying to plan alternative routes home. At least she knew she could walk from here, no matter how bad it was outside.

The sky had darkened rapidly, with thick

grey clouds hanging overhead, continuing their deluge of snow.

Snow. It was such a pretty thing. The kind of thing you spent hours cutting out of paper as a kid, trying to make a snowflake. Then sticking on a blue piece of card and putting on the classroom wall or attaching to a piece of string and hanging from the Christmas tree.

It didn't look like this in the storybooks. Thick wads of snow piled at the edges of the street, blanketing the road and stopping all traffic. The whiteness gone, leaving mounds of grey, icy sludge.

There was a creaking noise behind her and across the street, followed by a flood of shouts. 'Move! Quickly!'

In slow motion she watched as a large pile of snow slowly slid from a roof four storeys above the street. The people beneath were hurrying past, blissfully unaware of what was happening above their heads.

It was like a slow-moving action scene from a movie. All the inevitability of knowing what was about to happen without being able to intervene. Her breath caught in her throat. A woman in a red coat. A little boy. An elderly couple walking hand in hand. A few businessmen with their coat collars turned up, talking intently on their phones.

There was a flash of navy blue. The woman in the red coat and little boy were flung rapidly from the sidewalk into the middle of the empty street. The elderly couple pressed up against a glass shop window as some frantic shouts alerted the businessmen.

The snow fell with a thick, deafening thump. A cloud of powdered snow lifting into the air and a deluge of muddy splatters landing on her face.

Then, for a few seconds, there was silence. Complete silence.

It was broken first by the whimpers of a crying child—the little boy who had landed in the road. Seconds later chaos erupted. Onlookers dashed to the aid of the woman and small child, helping them to their feet and ushering them over to a nearby coffee shop. A few moments later someone guided the elderly couple from under the shelter of the shop's awning where they had been protected from the worst of the deluge.

'Where's the cop?'

'What happened to the cop?'

A policeman. Was that who had dived to the rescue? Her eyes caught the flicker of the blue lights of the NYPD car parked on the street. It was such a common sight in New York that she'd stopped registering them.

Some frantic digging and a few choice expletives later and one of New York's finest, along with one of the businessmen, emerged from the snow.

Someone jolted her from behind and her feet started to automatically move along the sludgy sidewalk. There was nothing she could do here.

Her own heart was pounding in her chest. Fat use she would be anyway. She didn't have a single medical skill to offer, and the street was awash with people rushing to help. She could see the cop brushing snow angrily from his uniform. He looked vaguely familiar but she couldn't place him. He was holding his wrist at a funny angle and looking frantically around, trying to account for all the people he had tried to save.

A tissue appeared under her nose. 'Better give your face a wipe,' said another woman, gesturing towards her mud-splattered coat, shoes and face.

Carrie turned towards the nearest shop window and did a double take. She looked like something the cat had dragged in. 'Thanks,' she muttered as she lifted the tissue to her face, smudging the mud further across her cheek. Her bright green coat was a write-off. The dry-clean-only label floated inside her mind. No dry-cleaning in the world could solve this mess.

She stared up at the darkening sky. It was time to go home. Whether it felt like home or not.

Daniel Cooper coughed and spluttered. His New York skyline had just turned into a heavy mix of grey-white snow. Wasn't snow supposed to be light and fluffy? Why did it feel as if someone were bench-pressing on top of him? A pain shot up his arm. He tried his best to ignore it. *Mind over matter. Mind over matter.*

There was noise above him, and shuffling. He spluttered. Snow was getting up his nose. It was strange being under here. Almost surreal.

He didn't feel as if he was suffocating. The snow wasn't tightly packed around his face. He just couldn't move. And Dan didn't like feeling as if things were out of his control.

The scuffling above him continued and then a few pairs of strong arms pulled him upwards from the snow. His head whipped around, instantly looking to see if the mother and child were safe.

There. On the other side of the sidewalk. He could see the flash of her red coat. Throwing them towards the street probably hadn't been the wisest move in the world, but the street was deep in snow, with not a car in sight. People were crowded around them but they were both safe, if a little shocked. The woman lifted her head and caught his eye. One of her hands was wrapped around her son, holding him close to her side, the other hand she placed on her chest. She looked stunned, her gaze registering the huge mound of snow that they would have been caught under, the horror on her face apparent. *Thank you,* she mouthed at him.

He smiled. The air left his lungs in a whoosh of relief. Snow was sticking to the back of his neck, turning into water that was trickling down his spine. As if he weren't wet enough already.

The elderly couple. Where were they? And why was his wrist still aching so badly? He spun back around. The elderly couple were being escorted across the street towards a side-walk café. Thank goodness. He gave a shiver. He didn't even want to think about the broken bones they could have suffered—or the head injuries.

'Buddy, your wrist, are you hurt?' A man in a thick wool coat was standing in front of him, concern written all over his face.

Dan looked down. The thing he was trying to ignore. The thing he was trying to block from his mind. He glanced at the pile of snow he'd been buried under. There, in amongst the debris, were some slate shingles. Who knew how many had fallen from the roof above. He was just lucky that one had hit his wrist instead of his head.

Darn it. His eyes met those of the concerned citizen in front of him. 'I'll see about it later,' he muttered. 'I'm sure it will be fine. Let me make sure everyone's okay.'

The man wrinkled his brow. 'They've called an ambulance for the other guy.' He nodded towards the sidewalk, where one of the businessmen was sitting, looking pale-faced and decidedly queasy. Truth be told, he felt a little like that himself. Not that he'd ever let anyone know.

He tried to brush some of the snow from his uniform. 'Who knows how long the ambulance will take to get here. We might be better taking them to be checked over at the clinic on Sixteenth Street.' He signalled across the street to another cop who'd appeared and was crossing quickly towards him. 'Can you talk to dispatch and see how long it will take the ambulance to get here?'

The other cop shook his head and threw up his hands. 'The whole city is practically shut down. I wouldn't count on anyone getting here any time soon.' He looked around him.

'I'll check how many people need attention—' he nodded towards Dan '—you included, then we'll get everyone round to the clinic.' He rolled his eyes. 'It's gonna be a long shift.'

Dan grimaced. The city was in crisis right now. People would be stranded with no way of getting home. Flights were cancelled. Most of the public transport was shutting down. How much use would he be with an injured wrist?

A prickle of unease swept over him as he looked at the streets crowded with people. He should be doing his job, helping people, not sloping off to a clinic nearby.

He hated that. He hated the elements that were out of his control. He looked at the crowds spilling out onto the sidewalk from Fourteenth Street station and took a deep breath.

Things could only get worse.

Carrie stared out of the window. The sun had well and truly disappeared and the streets were glistening with snow. Not the horrible sludge she'd trudged through earlier—but freshly fallen, white snow. The kind that looked almost inviting from the confines of a warmly lit apartment.

Her stomach rumbled and she pressed her hand against it. Thank goodness Mr Meltzer lived above his store. Every other store in the area had pulled their shutters and closed. She glanced at the supplies on the counter. Emergency milk, water, bread, bagels, cheese, macaroni and chocolate. Comfort food. If she was going to be snowed in in New York she had every intention of eating whatever she liked. It would probably do her some good. After the stress of last year she still hadn't regained the weight she'd lost. Gaining a few pounds would help fill out her clothes. It was so strange that some women wanted to diet away to almost nothing—whereas all she wanted was to get her curves back again.

Her ears pricked up. There it was again. That strange sound that had brought her to the window in the first place. This apartment was full of odd noises—most of which she'd gotten used to. Rattling pipes with trapped air, squeaking doors and floorboards, sneaky unexplained drafts. But this one was different. Was it coming from outside?

She pressed her nose up against the glass, her breath steaming the space around her. The street appeared deathly quiet. Who would venture out on a night like this? The twenty-four-hour news channels were full of *Stay indoors. Don't make any journeys that aren't absolutely necessary.* Anyone, with any sense, would be safely indoors.

She pushed open the window a little, letting in a blast of cold air. Thank goodness for thermal jammies, bed socks and an embossed dressing gown.

She held her breath and listened. There it was again. It was like a mew. Was it a cat? Downstairs, in the apartment underneath, she could hear the faint thump of music. It must be the cop. He obviously wouldn't be able to hear a thing. She didn't even know his name. Only that he must be a cop because of the uniform he wore. Tall, dark and handsome. But he hadn't looked in her direction once since she'd arrived.

Who had left their cat out on a night like this? Her conscience was pricked. What should she do? Maybe it was just a little cat confused by the snow and couldn't find its way home. Should she go downstairs and investigate? She glanced down at her nightwear. It would only take a few seconds. No one would see her.

She could grab the cat from the doorway and bring it in for the night. Maybe give it a little water and let it curl in front of the fire. A cat. The thought warmed her from the inside out. She'd never had a cat before. It might be nice to borrow someone else's for the night and keep it safe. At least she would have someone to talk to.

She opened her door and glanced out onto the

landing. Everyone else was safely ensconced in their apartments. Her feet padded down the flights of stairs, reaching the doorway in less than a minute. She unlocked the heavy door of the brownstone and pulled it open.

No.

It couldn't be.

She blinked and shut the door again. Fast.

Her heart thudded against her chest. One. Two. Three. Four. Five. Her brain was playing horrible tricks on her. Letting her think she was safe and things were safely locked away before springing something out of the blue on her.

Maybe she wasn't even awake. Maybe she'd fallen asleep on the sofa upstairs, in front of the flickering fire, and would wake up in a pool of sweat.

One. Two. Three. Four. Five.

She turned the handle again, oh-so-slowly, and prayed her imagination would get under control. Things like this didn't happen to people like her.

This time her reaction was different. This time the cold night air was sucked into her lungs with a force she didn't think she possessed. Every hair on her body stood instantly on end—and it wasn't from the cold.

It was a baby. Someone had left a baby on her doorstep.

CHAPTER TWO

FOR A SECOND, Carrie couldn't move. Her brain wouldn't compute. Her body wouldn't function.

Her ears were amplifying the sound. The little mew, mew, mew she'd thought she'd heard was actually a whimper. A whimper that was sounding more frightening by the second.

Her immediate instinct was to run—fast. Get away from this whole situation to keep the fortress around her heart firmly in place and to keep herself sheltered from harm. No good could come of this.

But she couldn't fight the natural instinct inside her—no matter how hard she tried. So she did what any mother would do: she picked up the little bundle and held it close to her chest.

Even the blanket was cold. And the shock of picking up the bundle chilled her.

Oh, no. The baby.

She didn't think. She didn't contemplate. She walked straight over to the nearest door—

the one with the thudding music—and banged loudly with her fist. 'Help! I need help!'

Nothing happened for a few seconds. Then the music switched off and she heard the sound of bare feet on the wooden floor. The door opened and she held her breath.

There he was. In all his glory. Scruffy dark hair, too-tired eyes and bare-chested, with only a pair of jeans clinging to his hips —and a bright pink plaster cast on his wrist. She blinked. Trying to take in the unexpected sight. His brow wrinkled. 'What the—?'

She pushed past him into the heat of his apartment.

'I need help. I found this baby on our doorstep.'

'A baby?' He looked stunned, then reached over and put a hand around her shoulders, pulling her further inside the apartment and guiding her into a chair next to the fire.

'What do I do? What do I do with a baby? Why would someone do this?' She was babbling and she couldn't help it. She was in a strange half-naked man's apartment in New York, with an abandoned baby and her pyjamas on.

This really couldn't be happening.

Her brain was shouting messages at her. But

she wasn't listening. She couldn't listen. *Get out of here*.

She stared down at the little face bundled in the blanket. The baby's eyes were screwed shut and its brow wrinkled. Was it a girl? Or a boy? Something shifted inside her. This was hard. This was so hard.

She shouldn't be here. She absolutely shouldn't be here. She was the last person in the world qualified to look after a baby.

But even though her brain was screaming those thoughts at her, her body wasn't listening. Because she'd lifted her hand, extended one finger and was stroking it down the perfect little cold cheek.

Dan Cooper's day had just gone from unlucky to ridiculous. He recognised her. Of course he recognised her. She was the girl with the sad eyes from upstairs.

But now she didn't look sad. She looked panicked.

He was conscious that her gaze had drifted across his bare abdomen. If she hadn't been banging on the door so insistently he would have pulled on a shirt first. Instead, he tried to keep his back from her line of vision as he grabbed the T-shirt lying across the back of his sofa.

He looked back at her. Now she didn't look panicked. She'd stopped babbling. In fact, she'd stopped talking completely. Now she just sat in front of the fire staring at the baby. She looked mesmerised.

His cop instinct kicked into gear. *Please don't let her be a crazy.* The last thing he needed today was a crazy.

He walked over and touched her hand, kneeling down to look into her eyes. He'd heard some bizarre tales in his time but this one took the biscuit. 'What's your name?'

She gave him only a cursory glance—as if she couldn't bear to tear her eyes away from the baby. 'Carrie. Carrie McKenzie. I live upstairs.'

He nodded. The accent drew his attention. The apartment upstairs was used by a business in the city. They often had staff from their multinational partners staying there. His brain was racing. He'd seen this girl, but had never spoken to her. She always looked so sad—as if she had the weight of the world on her shoulders.

He racked his brain. Had she been pregnant? Would he have noticed? Could she have given birth unaided upstairs?

His eyes swept over her. Pyjamas and a dressing gown. Could camouflage anything.

He took a deep breath. Time was of the essence here. He had to ask. He had to cover all the bases. 'Carrie—is this your baby?'

Her head jerked up. 'What?' She looked horrified. And then there was something—something else. 'Of course not!'

A feeling of relief swept over him. He'd been a cop long enough to know a genuine response when he saw one. Thank goodness. Last thing he needed right now was a crazy neighbour with a baby.

He reached over and pulled the fleecy blanket down from around the baby's face. The baby was breathing, but its cheeks were pale.

The nearest children's hospital was Angel's, all the way up next to Central Park. They wouldn't possibly be able to reach there in this weather. And it was likely that the ambulance service had ground to a halt. He had to prioritise. Even though he wasn't an expert, the baby seemed okay.

He stood up. 'How did you find the baby?'

Her brow wrinkled. 'I heard a noise. I thought it was a cat. I came downstairs to see.'

He couldn't hide the disbelief in his voice. 'You thought a baby was a cat?'

Her blue eyes narrowed as they met his. His tone had obviously annoyed her. 'Well, you know, it was kinda hard to hear with your music blaring.'

He ignored the sarcasm, even though it humoured him. Maybe Miss Sad-Eyes had some spunk after all. 'How long since you first heard it?' This was important. This was really important.

She shook her head. 'I don't know. Five minutes? Maybe a little more?'

His feet moved quickly. He grabbed for the jacket that hung behind the door and shoved his bare feet into his baseball boots.

She stood up. 'Where are you going? Don't leave me alone. I don't know the first thing about babies.'

He turned to her. 'Carrie, someone left this baby on our doorstep.' His eyes went to the window, to the heavy snow falling on the window ledge as he slid his arms into his jacket. 'Outside, there could be someone in trouble. Someone could be hurt. I need to go and check.'

She bit her lip and glanced at the baby before giving a small cursory nod of her head. He stepped outside into the bitter cold, glancing both ways, trying to decide which way to go. There was nothing in the snow. Any tracks that had been left had been covered within minutes; the snow was falling thick and fast.

He walked to the other side of the street and looked over at their building. Why here? Why had someone left their baby here?

There were some lights on in the other apartment buildings on the street. But most of the lights were in the second or third storeys. Theirs was the only building with lights on in the first floor. It made sense. Someone had wanted this baby found quickly.

He walked briskly down the street. Looking for anything—any sign, any clue. He ducked down a few alleyways, checking behind Dumpsters, looking in receded doorways.

Nothing. Nobody.

He turned and started back the other way. Checking the alleys on the other side of the street and in the opposite direction. His feet moving quickly through the sludgy snow.

He should have stopped and pulled some socks on. The thin canvas of his baseball boots was soaked through already. The temperature must have dropped by several degrees since the sun had gone down. He'd only been out here a few minutes and already he was freezing.

He looked up and his heart skipped a beat. Carrie was standing at his window, holding the baby in her arms. There was a look of pure desperation on her face—as if she were willing him to find the mother of this child.

It was a sight he'd never expected to see. A woman, holding a child, in his apartment. She'd pulled up his blinds fully and the expanse of the apartment he called home was visible behind her. His large, lumpy but comfortable sofa. His grandmother's old high-back chair. His kitchen table. His dresser unit. His kitchen worktop. The picture hanging above the fireplace.

Something niggled at him. His apartment was his space. He'd rarely ever had a relationship that resulted in him 'bringing someone over'. He could count on one hand the number of girlfriends who'd ever made it over his doorway. And even then it seemed to put them on an automatic countdown to disaster.

He didn't really do long-term relationships. Oh, he dated—but after a few months, once they started to get that hopeful look in their eyes, he always found a way to let them down gently. They eventually got the message. It was better that way.

So seeing Carrie standing in his apartment with a baby in her arms took the wind clean out of his sails. The sooner all this was over with, the better.

Still, she was cute. And even better—from London. She'd have no plans to stay around here. Maybe a little flirting to pass the time?

He gave himself a little shake and had another look around. There was no one out here. The streets were completely empty.

It was so funny being on the outside looking

in. He loved his home. He cherished it. But he'd never really taken a moment to stand outside and stare in—to see what the world must see on their way past if he hadn't pulled the blinds. His grandmother had left it to him in her will and he knew how lucky he was. There was no way a single guy on a cop's salary could have afforded a place like this.

But it was his. And he didn't even owe anything on it. All he had to do was cover the bills.

A little thought crept into his mind. He hadn't quite pulled the blinds fully tonight. He just hadn't gotten round to it. Was that why someone had left their baby here?

Did they see into his home and think it would be a safe place to leave a baby?

It sent a shudder down his spine. The thought that a few minutes ago someone could have been out here having those kind of thoughts.

The snowfall was getting even heavier—he could barely see ten feet in front of him. This was pointless. He was never going to find any clues in this weather. He had to concentrate on the immediate. He had to concentrate on the baby.

He hurried back into the apartment. Carrie turned to face him. 'Nothing?' The anxiety in her voice was obvious. Was she just a concerned citizen? Or was it something else?

He shook his head and pulled off his jacket, hanging it back up behind the door.

He walked over to where she was standing at the window and had another quick look out into the deserted street, searching for something, anything—a shadow, a movement. But there was nothing. Just the silence of the street outside.

He stood next to her, watching the way she cradled the baby in her arms. She was holding the baby, but he could sense she was uneasy. She'd said she didn't know the first thing about babies—well, neither did he. And in a snowstorm like this, it was unlikely they could get any help.

Most of the people who stayed around here were professionals. He couldn't think of a single family that stayed on this street. There were a couple of older people who had lived here for years. Mrs Van Dyke upstairs, but her family had long since moved away. There really wasn't anyone they could call on for help.

He watched her. The way her blue eyes were fixed on the face of the baby, still swaddled in its blanket. It was then he noticed the way her arms were trembling. It was slight—ever so slight. Making her chestnut curls waver and the pink flush of her cheeks seem heated.

She was beautiful. Now that he was close

enough to take a good look at her, Carrie Mc-
Kenzie was beautiful. Even if she didn't know
it herself. Even with the realm of sadness in
her blue eyes. He wondered what they looked
like when they were happy. Did they sparkle,
like the sun glinting off a turquoise-blue sea?

They were standing too close. He was sure
his warm breath must be dancing across her
skin. He could smell the orange scent of her
bath oils, still present on her skin. He liked it.
It was nicer than the cloying scent of some per-
fumes that women wore. The ones that prickled your nose from the other side of the room.
This was like a warm summer's day. Here, in
his living room, in the middle of a snowstorm
in New York.

She looked up at him with those sad blue
eyes. She didn't pull away from him. She didn't
seem to think he had invaded her personal
space. It was quite unnerving. He couldn't remember the last time he'd been this close to a
beautiful woman in his apartment—and certainly not one in her nightwear.

A smile danced across his face. If he'd ever
pictured a woman in his apartment in her nightwear it certainly hadn't been in fluffy pyjamas
and bed socks. She blinked and it snapped him
out of his wayward thoughts and back to the
current situation.

'I don't even know your name,' she whispered.

Wow. He hadn't even introduced himself. What kind of a New Yorker was he that his neighbour didn't even know his name? His grandma would kill him for his lack of manners and hospitality.

Why hadn't he ever introduced himself? Was it because he was so used to the constant flow of traffic up above him that he hadn't thought it worth his while? The thought shamed him. Because this woman definitely looked as if she could do with a friend. 'Dan. Daniel Cooper.'

'Daniel,' she repeated, as if she were trying to associate his face with the name. Her lips curled upwards. 'It's nice to meet you, Daniel,' she whispered, her gaze steady on his. 'Even if I am barely dressed.' He liked that about her. Even though her arms were trembling and she was clearly out of her depth, she could still look him clear in the eye and make a joke at her own expense.

The baby let out a whimper, reminding them of its presence, and he jerked back to reality. 'Maybe it's time to find out whether we've had a boy or a girl.' He raised his eyebrows at her and held out his hands to take the bundle from her.

It only took a few seconds to relieve her of

the weight. There was a noticeable sigh of relief in her shoulders as she handed the baby over.

He walked closer to the fire and unwound the little blanket. His cast made it awkward. There were no baby clothes underneath—no diaper. Just a little wrinkled towel. Carrie let out a gasp, lifting her hand to her mouth at the sight of a piece of string and a barely shrivelled umbilical cord.

Dan sucked in a deep breath. 'Well, like I said, I'm no expert but I guess this means we have a newborn.' A million thoughts started to flood into his head but he tried to push them aside. 'And I guess I should say congratulations, we've got a boy.' He rewrapped the blanket and lifted the little one onto his shoulder, trying to take in the enormity of the situation.

'I have a friend who works at Angel's, the children's hospital. Let me give her a call.'

'Her?'

He lifted his head. It was just the way she said the word *her*. As if it implied something else entirely.

'Yes. She's a paediatrician. Since neither of us know what we're doing and we can't get any immediate help, I guess she's the best bet we've got.'

He walked over to the phone and dialled quickly, putting the phone onto speaker as he adjusted the baby on his shoulder, away from his cast. 'Can you page Dr Adams for me? Tell her it's Sergeant Cooper and it's an emergency. Thanks.'

It only took a few seconds to connect. 'Dan? What's up?'

The relief he felt was instant. Shana was the best kids' doctor that he knew. She would tell him exactly what to do.

'Hi, Shana. I've got a bit of a problem. I've had a baby dumped on my doorstep and from the looks of it, it's a newborn.'

'What?' He could hear the incredulous tone in her voice. 'In this weather?'

'Exactly.'

Shana didn't mess around. She was straight down to business. 'Is the baby breathing?'

'Yes.'

'How cold? Do you have a thermometer? What's the baby's colour? And how is it responding?'

Carrie burst in. 'We think he was outside for just over five minutes. His skin was cold when I brought him in—and he was pale. But he's started to warm up. He looks pinker now.' Her brow was furrowed. 'Do you have a thermometer, Dan?' She was shaking her head. 'I don't.'

'Who's that?'

Daniel cleared his throat. 'That's Carrie, my

neighbour from upstairs. It was she who heard the baby crying. And no, Shana, we don't have a thermometer.'

'No matter. Crying? Now that's a good sign. That's a positive.'

Carrie shook her head. 'Not crying exactly, more like a whimper.'

'Any noise is good noise. You said he's a newborn. Is the cord still attached? Is it tied off?'

'Yes, it's tied with a piece of string. Doesn't look the cleanest. But the baby was only wrapped up in a blanket. No clothes. No diaper.'

'Sounds like no preparation. I wonder if the mother had any prenatal care. Does the baby look full term?'

Daniel shrugged and looked at Carrie, who shook her head and mouthed, *I don't know.*

'To be honest, Shana, neither of us are sure. I guess he looks okay. What does a full-term baby look like?'

'Does he have a sucking reflex? Is he trying to root?'

'What? I have no idea what you're talking about.' He was trying hard not to panic. This was all second nature to Shana. These types of questions were the ones she asked day in, day out. To him it all sounded like double Dutch.

They could hear the sound of muffled laughter at the other end of the phone. 'One of you, scrub your hands thoroughly under the tap then brush your finger around the side of the baby's mouth. I want to know if he turns towards it, as if he's trying to breastfeed or bottlefeed.'

Daniel nodded at Carrie, who walked over to the sink and started scrubbing her hands. 'Give us a second, Shana.'

Carrie dried her hands and then walked back over and lifted her finger hesitantly to the side of the baby's mouth. It took a few gentle brushes to establish that the little guy was reacting to her touch, turning towards it and opening his mouth.

'Yes, Shana. We think he is responding.'

'Good. That's a sign that he's around full term.' She gave an audible sigh. 'Okay, Daniel, you're not going to like this.'

'What?' Did she think something was wrong with the baby?

'There's no way I can send anyone from Angel's to get that baby. Our emergency room is packed and the roads around us are completely impassable. And from the weather report it's going to be like that for a few days.'

'Is that the good news or the bad news?' The mild feeling of panic was starting to rise.

Shana let out a laugh. 'Probably both. It sounds as if your baby is doing okay. Thank goodness. He will need a proper assessment as soon as possible. I'll put the necessary call in to social services, but they are on the other side of the city from you and everyone is in crisis right now. It will be a few days before they get to you. In the meantime the first thing you need to do is feed the little guy. Do you have somewhere local you can get some supplies?'

Blank. His brain had instantly gone blank. He'd never had any reason to look for baby supplies before. Where on earth would he get them?

Carrie touched his arm. 'Mr Meltzer stays above his store. I'm sure he'll have some powdered baby milk and diapers we can buy.'

Instant relief, followed by a sickening feeling in the pit of his stomach. 'Shana, you can't seriously expect us to look after a baby. Me, Shana? Seriously?'

'Daniel Cooper, you're one of the most responsible guys I know. I can't think of a single other person I would trust with a newborn baby right now. You're like any brand-new parent. None of them have experience. They just learn as they go. You'll need to do the same.'

'But they have nine months to get used to the idea. They read dozens of books about what to do—'

'And you have your own personal paediatrician at the other end of a phone. Not that I think you'll need me.'

Daniel could feel his heartbeat quicken in his chest. He wasn't afraid—not really. As a New York cop he'd dealt with most things in life. He'd had a gun pulled on him, a knife—on more than one occasion. He'd stopped a young girl from being abducted once, and managed to resist the temptation of doing what he really wanted to the potential kidnapper. He'd even talked a guy down from the edge of a rooftop before. But this? Looking after a baby? Why did it seem more intimidating than anything else?

'Shana, I don't think I'm the best person for the job.'

'Why not? You're practical. You're resourceful. And right now you're the best that baby's got.' She was beginning to sound exasperated. Angel's must be under an enormous amount of pressure right now, and he really didn't want to add to it. 'You've even got some help from your neighbour.'

He glanced over at Carrie, who was shaking her head frantically. *No,* she was mouthing.

'Suck it up, Daniel—and call me if you have any problems.' There was a click at the other end of the phone.

Carrie's chin was practically bouncing off

the floor. 'Suck it up, Daniel? Suck it up? That's what she says to you?' Her voice was getting higher pitched by the second and the baby was starting to squirm in his arms, reacting to the noise.

Reactions? Was that a good sign, too? He really didn't have a clue.

He shrugged. 'She's my best friend's older sister. It isn't the first time Shana's told me to suck it up—and it won't be the last.' He walked over to the sofa and sank down onto the cushions. This little guy weighed more than he thought. Or maybe it was just because he couldn't swap him between his arms.

'I'm going to have to put a call in to the station, to let my captain know about the abandoned baby.'

Carrie sagged down next to him on the sofa. She shook her head and squeezed her eyes shut. 'I know we've just met, Daniel, but I'm sorry. I just can't help you with this. I can't do it. Babies—' she hesitated '—they're just not my thing. I won't be any help anyway. I don't know a thing about babies.'

He stared at her. Hard. 'You've got to be joking, right?'

Her eyes opened and widened. It was clear she was instantly on the defence. 'No. Why?'

He shook his head in disbelief. 'You turn up

at my door with a baby, and now you're expecting to dump it on me in the middle of a snowstorm.'

When he said the words out loud they were even worse than the thoughts in his head.

Her face paled. 'But I...'

'I nothing.' A grin appeared on his face. 'Suck it up, Carrie.'

She drew back from him and he could sense her taking some deep breaths. 'It's not quite like that.'

He shook his head. There was no way she was leaving him high and dry. He waved his cast at her. 'What am I supposed to do? How am I supposed to bath a baby with one of these? Sure, I can probably manage to feed a baby and make up some bottles. But be practical, Carrie. I'm hardly the ideal babysitter right now.' He could see her staring at his pink cast and trying to work things out in her head. 'Least you can do is give me some help.'

Her cheeks flushed with colour, as if she'd just realised how mean it looked to walk away.

She pointed at his cast. 'How did you end up with that anyway? And what made you pick a pink cast?'

He snorted. '*Pick* isn't the word I would choose. There was an accident earlier today, a tonne of snow fell off a roof and I got trapped underneath it pushing people out of the way.'

Her eyes widened. 'On Fourteenth Street? That was you?'

He sat up a little straighter. 'How do you know about that?'

'I was there. I saw it happen.' She tilted her head to the side and stared at him again. 'I didn't realise it was you—I mean, I didn't know you.' She reached over and touched his cast. 'I remember. I remember seeing you hold your wrist at a funny angle. I guess it's broken, then?'

He nodded.

'And the pink?'

He smiled. 'It seems that today was the biggest day in the world for fractures at the clinic on Sixteenth Street.' He waved his wrist. 'Pink was the only colour they had left.'

She started to laugh. 'I can just imagine the look on your face when they told you that.'

He started to laugh, too. 'I was less than impressed. The air might have been a little blue.'

'Not pink?'

'Definitely not pink.'

She shook her head. 'That was really scary. I just remember the noise and the shouts. What about that woman in the red coat and her little boy? And that elderly couple?'

She really had been there. And she could remember the details. The lady could be a cop. 'All checked out and okay. One of the businessmen twisted his ankle and the other was being assessed for a head injury. He kept being sick.'

'Wow. Thank goodness you were there.'

Her words struck a chord with him. He hadn't really thought about that. He'd been too angry at breaking his wrist and being out of action for the NYPD. He hadn't really had time to stop to think about what could have happened to that elderly couple, or the woman and her young son.

A vision flashed in his eyes. The woman in the red coat cradling her son with one arm as if he was the most precious thing on earth. Then looking at him, with her hand on her heart, and mouthing, *Thank you*. He hadn't really had time to talk to her properly, but that one action had been more than enough for him. He didn't do this job for the thanks.

The little bundle shifted in his arms and started to whimper again. There was colour coming into the baby's cheeks and his tongue was starting to play around the edge of his mouth. He sighed. 'I guess our boy is getting hungry. I'll give Mr Meltzer a call and see if he can open the store so we can get some supplies. Know anything about making baby bottles?'

Carrie shook her head quite forcefully. 'I've told you—I can't help. This isn't my thing.'

But Dan was already on his feet, shifting his weight and moving the baby into her arms, whether she was ready or not. 'My computer's right next to you. Do an internet search while I'm gone.' He flicked through the nearby phone directory and punched a number into his phone. 'I'll only be five minutes.'

He grabbed his jacket and headed for the door again. What was her problem? He wasn't so chauvinistic that he expected all women to want to be mothers, but he did expect any responsible adult to help out in an emergency situation.

Maybe it was just the cop in him. Maybe his expectations of the average person were too high. But he'd seen the way she'd looked at the baby. She might not have experience, but she couldn't hide the tenderness in her eyes.

Maybe she was just uncomfortable with the pyjama situation. Maybe he should offer to let her go back upstairs and get changed.

He pressed the send button on his phone as he headed along the white street. Whatever it was, she'd better get over it quick. There was no way he was doing this on his own.

* * *

Carrie sat frozen on the sofa.

This wasn't happening. This couldn't be happening.

There was a weight pressed firmly against her chest. Like a huge dumb-bell just sitting there, taunting her to try and pull some air into her lungs.

He was scowling at her again. The baby. Nearly as much as Daniel Cooper had scowled at her when she'd tried to pull out all the lame excuses under the sun to get out of here.

It must make her seem like a bitch. But right now she didn't care.

She could feel tears starting to flood into her eyes. This was someone's precious baby. Someone's living, breathing, precious bundle. What on earth could happen in this life that would make you leave a baby on someone's doorstep in the middle of a snowstorm?

It wasn't fair. Life wasn't fair.

Last time she'd held a baby it hadn't been moving. Its little chest didn't have the rise and fall that this little boy's had. It didn't have the pink flush to its cheeks.

She blinked back the tears. The tightening in her chest was getting worse.

It.

A terrible term.

But she couldn't use any other right now. She couldn't think about her daughter. She couldn't think about Ruby McKenzie. She couldn't let that name invade her thoughts.

Because then she would spiral downwards. Then she would remember the nursery and pram. Then she would remember the routine check at the midwife's, followed by the urgent scan. Then she would remember the forty-eight-hour labour, with no cry of joy at the end of it.

Then she would remember the disintegration of her five-year relationship, as both of them struggled to cope with their bereavement.

The whimpering was getting worse, turning into full-blown screams.

She'd have given anything to hear the screams of her daughter. She'd have given anything to see her daughter screw up her face and let out a yell like that.

She shifted the baby onto her shoulder. Five minutes. Dan would be back in five minutes.

She put her hand on the keyboard of the computer and did a quick search. If she could keep her mind on something else, she could fight back the feelings. She could stop them from enveloping her. *How to sterilise and prepare bottles.*

She read the screen in front of her, scanning quickly. Her hand automatically moving and patting the baby on the back. She could do this. She could help him make a bottle and then leave.

He couldn't expect any more. She couldn't *give* any more.

She could feel herself pulling in—withdrawing inside herself. Turning into someone else. Stepping outside herself to a place where there was no hurt, no memories. Switching off.

It was the only way she'd coped before. And it was the only way she could cope now.

She glanced at the clock. Ten minutes maximum.

She could keep this face painted in place for ten minutes when he got back. That was how long it would take to sterilise the bottle, make up the powdered milk and leave him positioned on the sofa.

Her eyes registered something on the screen. Darn it! Cooled boiled water. How long did the water have to cool for before it was suitable to give a baby?

Maybe he'd only just boiled the kettle. She juggled the baby in her arms and walked over to the kitchen countertop, putting her hand on the side of the kettle. Stone cold. She picked it up and gave it a shake—and practically empty.

Nightmare.

She ran the tap and filled the kettle, putting

it back into position and flicking the switch for it to boil.

Then she felt it—and heard it.

That first little squelchy noise. Followed by a warm feeling where her hand was resting on the baby's bottom.

No nappy. This little boy had no nappy on.

Her heart sank like a stone as she felt the warm feeling spread across her stomach. Could this night really get any worse?

CHAPTER THREE

DAN ENDED THE CALL on his phone. His captain had let out the loudest, heartiest laugh he'd ever heard when he'd told him about the baby. It hadn't helped.

He could hear pandemonium in the background at the station. He should be there helping. Instead of doing a late-night recce for baby supplies.

Mr Meltzer, on the other hand, had been full of concern. Loading up supplies on the counter and waving his hand at Dan's offer of payment.

'If I help the little guy get a better start in life that's all I need.'

The words tormented him. Ground into him in a way they shouldn't. If only everyone felt like Mr Meltzer.

He pushed open the door to the apartment building and kicked the snow off his favourite baseball boots. They were really beyond repair.

Carrie was waiting and she pulled open the inside door. 'Did you get some milk?'

He nodded and dumped the bags on the counter.

'Wow, how much stuff did you get?'

He pulled his arms out of his jacket. 'Who knew a baby needed so much? Mr Meltzer just kept pulling things off his shelves and saying, "You better take some of that".'

Carrie tipped one of the bags upside down. 'Please tell me you got some nappies and dummies. We need both—now.'

'What? What are you talking about?'

She waved her hand in the air. 'Oh, you Americans. Nappies—diapers. And dummies— what do you call them? Pacifiers? He's starting to get restless and it will take a little time to sterilise the bottles.' She rummaged through the bags. 'You did get bottles, didn't you?'

'What's that smell?' He wrinkled his nose and caught sight of the expression on her face. 'Oh, no. You're joking. He can't have. He hasn't eaten yet.' He pulled out a pack of baby wipes. 'I take it we'll need these?'

She nodded. 'Do you have a towel we can lay him on? I'd say getting a nappy on the little guy is a priority.'

Dan walked over to the laundry cupboard and started throwing things about. 'I know I've

got a brand-new set of towels in here somewhere. My friend Dave just got married. He
was drowning in the things. Ah, here we are!'
He pulled out some navy blue towels and laid
one down on the rug, a little away from the fireplace. He glanced at his cast. It was more incon-
venient than he first thought—to say nothing
about the constant ache that was coming from
his wrist. 'Can you do this?'

He could see her taking a deep breath. 'Fine,'
she muttered through gritted teeth. She grabbed
the bag of diapers from the counter, along with
the wipes and some diaper sacks. 'Did you get
some cream?'

'Cream? What for?'

'For putting on the baby's bum, of course.
Everyone knows you put cream on a baby to
stop them from getting nappy rash.'

He shrugged his shoulders. 'Mr Meltzer
didn't seem to know—and he knew everything
else.' He pulled something from a second plastic bag. 'Look—ready-made formula in a carton. We've got the powdered stuff, too, but he
said this was ready to use.'

She scowled at him as she laid the baby down
on the fresh towel and peeled back the blanket.

'Eww!'

'Yuck!'

The smell was awful and filled the apartment

instantly. The baby, on the other hand, seemed to quite like the freedom the open blanket gave and started to kick his legs.

'How can all that stuff come from one tiny little thing?' He really wanted to pinch his nose shut.

Carrie was shaking her head, too, as she made a dive for the baby wipes. 'I have no idea, but the next one is yours.'

He looked at her in horror. 'No way.' He waved his pink cast again. 'Can you imagine getting a bit of that caught on here? It would stink forever. I would smell like this for the next six weeks.' He shook his head. 'At least you can wash your hands.'

Carrie was deep in concentration, wiping and thrusting the dirty wipes into the supposedly scented diaper sack. She pulled out one of the diapers and held it up. 'Well, at least you seemed to have got the right size.'

Dan bit his lip. 'Actually, there was a whole shelf of the things. Mr Meltzer picked them out.'

She raised her eyebrow. 'Can you ask him to come babysit, too, please? He seems to be the only person around here who knows anything about babies.'

'I tried. He wasn't buying it.'

Carrie positioned the diaper under the clean

little bottom and snapped the tapes into place. 'There, that's better. Pity the smell hasn't disappeared.' She picked up the blanket by the corner. 'This will need washing. Where's your machine?'

'In the basement.'

She let out a sigh. 'I don't get that about New York. Why does everyone have their washing machine in the basement?' She waved her hands around. 'You've plenty of room in here. Why isn't your washing machine in the kitchen? Everyone in London has their washing machine in their flat. You don't have to walk down miles of stairs to do the laundry.'

'Worried about leaving your underwear unguarded?'

There it was again. That cheeky element coming out. He couldn't help it. She seemed so uptight at times.

Just as he suspected, a pink colour flooded her cheeks. He could almost hear the ticking of her brain trying to find a way to change the subject quickly.

She nodded over to the counter. 'We need to sterilise the bottles.'

'I think he gave me some tablets for that.' Dan started to root around in one of the bags.

'He probably did, but according to the internet the bottles would need to be in the sterilising solution for thirty minutes. It only takes ten minutes if we boil them. That way you can use the ready-made formula and get it into him quicker.'

'What about one of these? Can we give him a pacifier in the meantime?'

Carrie shook her head. 'I think we need to sterilise them, too. And we need to use only cooled boiled water with the powdered milk. But I've no idea how long water takes to cool once you've boiled it. And I don't know whether we should put the milk in the fridge or keep it at room temperature—everyone seems to have a different opinion on the internet.' She was getting more harassed by the second, the words rattling out of her mouth and her face becoming more flushed. 'I told you—I'm not an expert in all this. I have no idea what I'm doing!'

Something clenched in his stomach. He could sense the feelings overwhelming her, and he had a whole host of some himself.

Deep down, having a woman in his apartment—without an expiry date—was freaking him out. But these weren't normal circumstances. He *needed* Carrie McKenzie's help. He couldn't do this on his own and right now he could sense she wanted to cut and run.

He was feeling a bit flustered himself. Flustered that some gorgeous Brit was in his space.

But this wasn't about him. This wasn't about Daniel Cooper and the fact he liked his own space. This wasn't about the fact his relationships only lasted a few months because he didn't want anyone getting comfortable in his home—comfortable enough to start asking questions. This was about a baby. A baby who needed help from two people.

So, he did what his grandma had always taught him. Her voice echoed in his head. *You get the best out of people when you compliment them—when you thank them for what they do.*

He reached over and touched Carrie's hand. She was getting flustered again, starting to get upset. 'Carrie McKenzie?' He kept his voice low.

'What?' she snapped at him.

Yep, he was right. Her eyes had a waterlogged sheen. She was just about to start crying.

He gave her hand a little squeeze. 'I think you're doing a great job.'

The world had just stopped because she wasn't really in it.

This was one of those crazy dreams. The kind that had your worst type of nightmare and a knight in shining armour thrown in, too. The kind that made no sense whatsoever.

She wasn't here. She wasn't awake.

Her earlier thought had been true. She was actually fast asleep on the sofa upstairs. She would wake up in a few minutes and this would all be over. This would all be something she could shrug off and forget about.

Except those dark brown eyes were still looking at her.

Still looking as if he understood a whole lot more than he was letting on. As if he'd noticed the fact she was seconds away from cracking and bursting into floods of tears.

But he couldn't, could he? Because he didn't really know her at all.

Daniel Cooper was an all-action New York cop. The kind of guy from a romance movie who stole the heroine's heart and rode off into the sunset with her. A good guy.

The kind of guy who looked after an abandoned baby.

She was trying to swallow. Her mouth was drier than a desert, and it felt as if a giant turtle had started nesting at the back of her throat.

She looked down to where his hand covered hers. It was nice. It *felt* nice.

And that was the thing that scared her most.

When was the last time someone had touched her like that? At the funeral? There had been a lot of hand squeezing then. Comfort. Reassurance. Pity.

Not the same as this.

He smiled at her. A crooked kind of smile, revealing straight white teeth.

A sexy kind of smile. The kind that could take her mind off the nightmare she was currently in.

There was a yelp from the towel. Dan moved his hand and looked down. 'I guess baby's getting hungry. I'll stick the bottles in the pot.'

Carrie left the baby on the towel and started to look through the bags on the counter. Five prepacked cartons of formula, two different kinds of powder, more dummies and a whole mountain's worth of baby wipes.

She folded her arms across her chest as she watched Dan dangle the bottles and teats from his fingertips into the boiling water. 'Clothes, Dan. What are we going to put on him?'

His brow wrinkled and he shook his head. 'Darn it, I knew I'd forgotten something. There weren't any baby clothes in the general store, and there's no place else around here that sells any. Can't we just leave him in the diaper?'

Carrie shook her head. 'Want me to do a search on that?' She started to pace. 'Don't you know anyone around here with kids who might still have some baby clothes? How long have you stayed here?'

He blinked and his lips thinned. As if he was

trying to decide how to answer the question. He averted his eyes and started busying himself with the coffee maker. 'I've lived here on and off my whole life. This was my grandma's place.'

'Was it?' She was surprised but it made perfect sense. After all, how did a young guy on a cop's salary afford a gorgeous brownstone West Village apartment? She looked around, starting to take in the decor of the place. There were a few older items that didn't look quite 'him'. A rocker pushed in the corner near the window, a small antique-style table just at the front door, currently collecting mail and keys, a dresser in the more modern-style kitchen. It was kind of nice, to see the old mixed in with the new. 'It's a lovely place. Big, too. You're a lucky guy.'

He made a noise. More like a snort. 'Yeah, I guess. Just born lucky, me.'

Carrie froze, not really knowing how to respond. What did that mean?

But he must have realised his faux pas because he changed the subject quickly. 'The ten minutes will be up soon. Once we've fed the little guy I'll go on up to Mrs Van Dyke's place. Her family used to stay here. She might have some things in storage we could use.'

'Mrs Van Dyke? Which one is she? Is she the one on the second floor who looks as if she came over on the Mayflower and is about six hundred years old?'

He raised his eyebrows. 'Watch it. According to her, her family were amongst the original Dutch settlers. And I don't think she's quite six hundred years old. She's as sharp as a stick, and she hasn't aged in the past twenty-five years.' He gave her a wink as he switched off the burner. 'Maybe you should ask her what cream she uses.'

Carrie picked up an unopened packet of pacifiers and tossed them at his head. They bounced off the wall behind him.

'Careful, careful, we've got a baby in the apartment. We don't want anything to hit him.' He glanced at his watch. 'On second thought, it's getting kind of late. Maybe it's too late to go knocking on Mrs Van Dyke's door.' His gaze was still fixed on the baby, lying on the floor, grizzling impatiently for his milk.

Carrie folded her arms as she stood next to him. 'You've got to be kidding. Mrs Van Dyke is up watching TV until four a.m. most nights. And I take it she's getting a little deaf, because I can't get to sleep in my apartment because of the *Diagnosis Murder* or *Murder, She Wrote* reruns that I hear booming across the hall. Seriously, the woman needs a hearing aid.'

'And seriously? She'll be far too proud to get one.'

There was something nice about that. The fact that he knew his elderly neighbour so well that he could tell exactly why she didn't have a hearing aid. 'So what was wrong with me, then?' She couldn't help it. The words just spilled out.

'What do you mean?'

'You obviously know your other neighbours well, but it was too much trouble to even say hello to me in the foyer.'

The colour flooded into his cheeks. Unflappable Dan was finally flapping. He could deal with a tonne of snow falling from a roof, he could deal with a baby dumped on his doorstep, but this? This was making him avert his eyes and struggle to find some words.

'Yeah, I'm sorry about that. I just assumed you were staying for only a few days. Most of the others seemed like ships that pass in the night.'

'I've been here two months, Dan. Eight long weeks—' she let out a little sigh '—and to be honest, this isn't the friendliest place I've ever stayed.'

He cringed. 'I can hear my grandmother shouting in my ear right now. Shaming me on my bad manners. I did see you—but you always looked like you had a hundred and one things on your mind. You never really looked in the mood to talk.'

This time Carrie felt like cringing. There was a reason Dan was a cop. He was good at reading people. Good at getting to the heart of the matter. And she had only herself to blame for this, because it was she who'd called him on his behaviour.

She gave a little shrug, trying to brush it off. 'Maybe a cheery good morning would have been enough.'

She walked over and lifted the pot, tipping the boiling water into the sink.

He appeared at her back, his chin practically resting on her shoulder, as he lifted the plastic bottles and teats out onto the worktop with a clean dish towel. 'You're right, Carrie. You're absolutely right. I should have said hello. I should have said good morning.'

She turned her head slightly. He wasn't quite touching her, but she could feel the heat emanating from his body. She wanted to step away, to jerk backwards, but her body wasn't letting her.

Her lips were curving into a smile—even though she was telling them not to—as she stared into those brown eyes again. It was nice. Being up close to someone again. His lips were only inches from hers. She wondered if he was having the same kind of thoughts she was. The kind of thoughts that made her forget there was a baby in the room…until he let out an angry wail from the floor.

They jumped back, both at the same time. She reached for one of the cartons. 'Do you have a pair of scissors?'

He opened a drawer, pulled out the scissors, snipped the edge of the carton and upended the contents into one of the cooled bottles. Carrie picked up one of the teats by the edge of its rim and placed it on the bottle, screwing it in place with the retaining ring.

The bottle sat on the middle of the counter and they stared at each other for a few seconds.

'Don't we need to heat the milk up now?'

She shook her head. 'According to the internet, room temperature is fine.'

'Oh, okay.'

Silence. And some deep breathing, followed by a whole host of screams from the floor. It was like a Mexican stand-off.

'So, who is going to do this?'

'You. Definitely you.'

'But what if I do it wrong?'

'What if I do it wrong? Don't you dare suggest that I can do it better because I'm a girl.'

He raised his eyebrows. 'Oh, I'd never refer to you as a girl.'

'Stop it. He's mad. Just feed him.' She opened one of the kitchen drawers and handed him a dish towel. 'Here, put this over you.'

'What do I need that for?'

'In case he pukes on you.'

'Ewww...'

Dan picked up the bottle, holding it between his hands as if it were a medical specimen. He squinted at the markings on the side of the bottle. 'How much do I give him?'

'I don't know.'

'Well, look it up on the internet while I start.'

Relief. Instant relief. She wasn't going to be left to feed the baby. She could sit on the other side of the room and do a search on the computer.

Dan picked up the baby from the floor and settled him on his lap, resting him in the crook of his arm that had his cast in place. He held the bottle with his other hand and brushed the teat against the baby's cheek.

There were some angry noises, and some whimpering, before finally the baby managed to latch on to the teat and suck—furiously.

Carrie was holding her breath on the other side of the room, watching with a fist clenched around her heart. A baby's first feed.

One of those little moments. The little moments that a parent should share with a child.

Daniel seemed equally transfixed. He glanced over at her. 'Wow. Just wow. Look at him go. He's starving.'

And he was. His little cheeks showed he was sucking furiously. But it was Dan who had her attention. The rapt look on his face, and the way the little body seemed to fit so easily, so snugly against his frame.

Her mouth was dry and the hairs were standing up on the back of her neck. Worse than that, she could feel the tears pooling around her eyes again.

What was wrong with her? This had nothing to do with her. Nothing to do with her situation. She shouldn't be feeling like this. She shouldn't be feeling as if she couldn't breathe and the walls were closing in around her.

But Dan looked so natural, even though he kept shifting in the chair. He looked as if he was born to do this. Born to be a father. Born to be a parent.

The thing that she'd been denied.

She glanced at the screen and stood up quickly.

She had to leave now, while he was trapped in his chair and before the tears started to fall. She needed some breathing space.

'You should stop after every ounce of milk, Dan. Take the bottle out and wind the baby. I'm sorry. I have to go.'

'What? Carrie? Wait a minute, what does *wind* mean? How do I know how much an ounce is?'

But she couldn't stop. She couldn't listen.

'Carrie? Come back.'

But her feet were already on the stairs, pounding their way back up to the sanctuary of her solitude.

CHAPTER FOUR

DAN STARED AT the wall. What had just happened?

One minute she seemed fine, next minute a bundle of nerves, ready to jump out of her skin at the slightest noise.

She'd caught him unawares. She'd caught him while he was in no position to run after her. Probably planned it all along.

Still, it wasn't as if she could go anywhere. The city was at a standstill and if this little guy started screaming she was right upstairs. Whether she liked it or not.

He shifted on the sofa. The little guy was feeding fast and furious. Was this normal?

He heard some rumbling, the noises of the milk hitting the baby's stomach. How much was an ounce anyway? And how on earth could he tell if the baby had drunk that much when the bottle was tipped up sideways? At this rate he was going to need Shana on speed dial. He glanced at the clock and let out a sigh.

This was going to be a long, long night.

Carrie slammed the apartment door behind her and slid down behind it. Her mind was on a spin cycle. She couldn't think a single rational thought right now.

What Dan must think of her.

She tried to take some slow, deep breaths. Anything to stop her heart clamouring in her chest. Anything to stop the cold prickle across her shoulder blades.

She sagged her head into her hands. *Calm down. Calm down.*

This was ridiculous. Avoiding babies for the past year was one thing. Body-swerving pregnant friends and brand-new mothers was almost understandable.

But this wasn't. She had to stop with the self-pity. She had to get some perspective here.

What would she have done if Dan hadn't been in the building?

There was no way she would have left that baby on the doorstep. No matter how hard the task of looking after him.

And if she'd phoned the police department and they couldn't send anyone out? What would she have done then?

She lifted her head from her hands. She would have had a five-minute panic. A five-minute feeling of *this can't be happening to me*.

Then what?

There was a creeping realisation in her brain. She pushed herself back up the door. Her breathing easing, her heartbeat steadying.

Then she would have sucked it up. She would have sucked it up and got on with it.

Because that was what any responsible adult would do.

She strode over to the bedroom, shedding her dressing gown and bed socks and pulling her pyjama top over her head. She found the bra she'd discarded earlier and fastened it back in place, pulling on some skinny jeans and a pink T-shirt.

Her pink baseball boots were in the bottom of her cupboard and she pushed her feet into them.

There. She was ready.

But her stomach started to flutter again.

The light in the bathroom flickered. Was the light bulb going to blow again? Which it seemed to do with an annoying regularity. She walked inside and ran the tap, splashing some cold water over her face.

She stared into the mirror, watching the drops of water drip off her face. Dan would have labelled her a nutjob by now. He probably wouldn't want her help any more.

But the expression on his face was imprinted on her brain. He'd looked stunned. As if he couldn't understand—but he wanted to.

She picked up the white towel next to the sink and dried off her face. Her make-up was right next to her. Should she put some on? Like some camouflage? Would it help her face him again?

Her fingers hesitated over the make-up bag. It was late at night. She'd been barefaced and in her pyjamas. He wouldn't expect anything else.

But it might give her the courage she needed. It might make her feel as if she had some armour to face the world.

She pulled out some mascara and a little cream blusher, rubbing some on to her cheeks and then a touch on her lips. There. She was ready.

She crossed the room in long strides before any doubts could creep into place. There was no point in locking her apartment door. She would only be down two flights of stairs.

She placed her hand on the balustrade, ready to go down, and then halted. The television was booming from the apartment across the hall. Mrs Van Dyke.

The neighbour she'd only glimpsed in passing and never spoken to. The neighbour who might have some baby supplies they could use.

She hesitated and then knocked loudly on the door. 'Mrs Van Dyke? It's Carrie from across the hall. Daniel Cooper sent me up.'

She waited a few minutes, imagining it might take the little old lady some time to get out of her chair and over to the door—praying she'd actually heard her above the theme tune from *Murder, She Wrote*.

She could hear the creaking of the floorboards and then the door opened and the old wizened face stared out at her. Oh, boy. She really could be six hundred years old.

'And what do you want, young lady?'

Carrie jerked back a little. She had such a strong, authoritative voice, it almost reminded her of her old headmistress back in London.

She took a deep breath. 'I'm sorry to disturb you, Mrs Van Dyke, but we found a baby on the doorstep and Dan said you might be able to help.'

As the words tumbled out of her mouth she knew she could have phrased it better. If this old dear keeled over in shock it would be all her fault.

But Mrs Van Dyke was obviously made of sterner stuff.

'Oh, dear. What a terrible thing to happen. What does Dan need?'

Just like that. No beating about the bush. No preamble. Just straight to the point. Wonderful.

'We got some things from Mr Meltzer's store. He opened it specially to help out. We've got nappies—I mean, diapers—and pacifiers and bottles and milk.'

There was a gleam of amusement in the old lady's eyes. 'Just as well. I doubt I would have had any of those.'

Carrie shook her head. 'Of course. I mean— what we don't have is any baby clothes. Or any clean blankets. Do you have anything like that? Dan wondered if you might have some things packed away.'

Mrs Van Dyke nodded slowly and opened the door a little wider. 'I might have a few things that you can use, but most of them will be at the back of my cupboards. Come in, and I'll see what I can do.'

Carrie stepped into the apartment and stifled her surprise. 'Wow. What a nice place you have here.'

Clutter. Everywhere.

The floor was clear, but that was pretty much it.

There was no getting away from it—Mrs Van Dyke was clearly a hoarder.

She gave a smile and stepped further, keeping her elbows tight in against her sides for fear of tipping something off one of the tables or shelves next to her.

On second thoughts, Mrs Van Dyke wasn't your typical hoarder. Not the kind you saw on TV with twelve skips outside their house so it could be emptied by environmental health.

There were no piles of papers, magazines or mail. In fact, the only newspaper she could see was clearly deposited in the trash. And all the surfaces in the apartment sparkled. There was no dust anywhere. Just…clutter. Things. Ornaments. Pictures. Photo frames. Wooden carvings. Tiny dolls. Ceramics. The place was full of them.

No wonder Dan had thought she might have something they could use.

'They're mementos. They're not junk. Everything holds a memory that's special to me, or my family.'

Carrie jumped. Mrs Van Dyke seemed to move up silently behind her. Had she been so obvious with her staring?

'Of course not,' she said quickly.

Mrs Van Dyke picked up the nearest ornament. 'My husband used to carve things. This one he gave me on our first anniversary. A perfect rose.'

Carrie bent down and looked closely. It really was a thing of beauty. She couldn't even see the marks where the wood had been whittled away—it was perfectly smooth.

'It's beautiful.'

Mrs Van Dyke nodded. 'Yes, it is.' She walked slowly through the apartment, pointing as she went. 'This was the globe he bought me at Coney Island. This was a china plate of my grandmother's—all the way from Holland. This—' she held up another carving, this time of a pair of hands interlinked, one an adult's and one a child's '—is what he carved for me after our son Peter died when he was seven.'

Carrie's hand flew to her mouth. 'Oh, I'm so sorry.'

Mrs Van Dyke ran her finger gently over the carving as she sat it back down. 'It shows that we'd always be linked together, forever.'

She reached a door and gestured to Carrie. 'This is my box room. This is where I keep most of my things.'

Carrie was still taken aback by her comment about her son, so she pushed the door open without really thinking. She let out a gasp of laughter. 'You're not joking—it *is* a box room.' And it was. Filled with boxes from floor to ceiling. But there was no randomness about the room. Every box was clearly labelled and facing the door, and there was a thin path between the boxes. Room enough for someone of slim build to slip through.

'The boxes you're looking for are near the back.' She touched Carrie's shoulder. 'Your baby—is it a boy or a girl?'

Just the way she said it—*your baby*—temporarily threw her for a second. It took her a moment to collect her thoughts. 'It's a boy. It's definitely a boy.'

Mrs Van Dyke nodded. 'Straight to the back, on the left-hand side somewhere, near the bottom, you'll find a box with David's name on it. And behind it, you might find something else that's useful.'

Carrie breathed in and squeezed through the gap. The labelling was meticulous, every item neatly catalogued. Did this really make Mrs Van Dyke a hoarder? Weren't those people usually quite disorganised and chaotic? Because Mrs Van Dyke was none of those things.

The box with David's baby things was almost at the bottom of a pile. Carrie knelt down and started to gingerly edge it out, keeping her eyes on the teetering boxes near the top. The whole room had the potential to collapse like dominoes—probably at the expense of Mrs Van Dyke, who was standing in the doorway.

She pushed her shoulder against the pile, trying to support some of the weight wobbling above her as she gave a final tug to get the box out.

In that tiny millisecond between the boxes above landing safely in place, still in their tower, she saw what was behind the stack and it made her catch her breath.

A beautifully carved wooden cradle.

She should have guessed. With all the other carefully carved items of wood in the apartment, it made sense that Mr Van Dyke would have made a cradle for his children. She weaved her way back through the piles, careful not to knock any with her box, before sitting it at the door next to Mrs Van Dyke. 'Do you want to have a look through this to see what you think might be appropriate?'

She chose her words carefully. Mrs Van Dyke had already revealed she'd lost one child; there might be items in this box that would hold special memories for her. Items she might not want to give away. 'I'll go and try and get the cradle.'

It took ten minutes of carefully inching past boxes, tilting the cradle one way then another, before she finally managed to get out of the room.

She sat the cradle on the floor. Mrs Van Dyke was sitting in a chair with the open box on her lap, setting things in neat piles next to her.

Now that she had the cradle in the light of the room she was able to appreciate how fine the carving was. The cradle actually rocked. Something Carrie hadn't seen in years. The wooden spindles were beautifully turned, with a variety of ducks and bunnies carved at either end on the outside of the crib. Something like this would cost a small fortune these days.

She ran her fingers over the dark woodwork. 'This is absolutely beautiful. It looks like the kind of thing you would see in a stately home. Did your husband really make this himself?'

Mrs Van Dyke's eyes lit up at the mention of her husband. She smiled proudly. 'Yes, he did. It took him nearly four months.' She leaned forward and touched the cradle, letting it rock gently. 'This held all five of my children. Just for the first few months—they quickly outgrew it.'

'Are you sure we can borrow it? It looks like a precious family heirloom.'

Mrs Van Dyke nodded. 'A cradle is only really a cradle when it holds a baby. That's its job. You'll bring it back, mind?'

Carrie nodded. 'Social services have been called—' she held out her hands '—but with the snowstorm it might be a few days before they can collect the baby.'

Mrs Van Dyke handed her a small pile of clothes. 'I'm sorry. I didn't keep too much.

There's some vests, socks and some hand-knitted cardigans. Oh, and a blanket.'

'These will be great. Thank you so much. I'll launder them and bring them back to you in a few days.' She fingered the edge of the intricately crocheted blanket. 'This is beautiful and it looks brand new. Are you sure we can use this?'

Mrs Van Dyke smiled and shook her head. 'It's not new. I made a new blanket for every child. This was the final one. You're welcome to use it.'

Carrie smiled gratefully. 'Thank you, it's gorgeous and I'm sure it will be perfect.' She sat the clothes inside the cradle and picked it up. 'I'm sure Dan will be really grateful to you, too. If there's anything you need in the next few days be sure to let us know. We can ask Mr Meltzer to open his store again.'

Mrs Van Dyke shook her head. 'I'll be fine. My pantry is well stocked.'

Carrie walked over to the door. 'Thanks, Mrs Van Dyke.' She opened the door and gave a little smile. 'You have a beautiful home here.'

Mrs Van Dyke smiled. 'And you're welcome in it any time.'

Carrie juggled the cradle in her hands and closed the door behind her quietly.

Wow. Not what she'd expected at all.

Mrs Van Dyke was lovely, a real pleasure to be around. And she could imagine that Mrs Van Dyke could regale Carrie with hundreds of stories about her life and her family.

She thought of the little carving of a mother's and child's hands interlinked. It was heartbreaking—and it was beautiful. It hadn't felt right to ask any questions about her son Peter. She'd only just met Mrs Van Dyke and that would be intrusive.

But she'd felt the *connection*. The connection that only another mother who had lost a child could feel.

Obviously she hadn't said anything to Mrs Van Dyke. The woman hardly knew her. But that little feeling in the pit of her stomach had told her that this woman would be able to understand exactly how she felt.

Their circumstances were obviously different. Mrs Van Dyke had spent seven years loving and cherishing her son, getting to know his thoughts and quirks, growing together as mother, child and part of a family. Carrie had missed out on all that.

She'd spent seven months with her hands on her growing stomach, with a whole host of hopes and expectations for her child. In her head she'd been making plans for the future. Plans that involved a child.

None of those plans had been for a future without her daughter.

Her hands were starting to shake a little. Was it from the weight in her hands—or was it from the thoughts in her head?

A cradle is only really a cradle when it holds a baby.

How true.

She'd loved the white cot she'd bought for her daughter. But it hadn't been nearly as beautiful as this one. It had been dismantled and packed off to the nearest charity shop, along with the pram, because she couldn't bear to look at them.

Hopefully some other baby had benefitted from them.

Carrie walked down the stairs carefully, making sure she didn't bang the cradle on the way. Who knew what Dan would say to her? She wouldn't be surprised if he let rip with some choice words.

Her ears pricked up. Crying—no, wailing. The baby was screaming at the top of his lungs. Her steps quickened and she pushed open Dan's door with her shoulder.

'Dan, what on earth is going on?'

Dan's ears were throbbing. Weren't there environmental laws about noise? No one seemed to have told this little guy.

He changed him over to the other shoulder. This had been going on for the past fifteen minutes. What on earth had gone wrong?

He screwed up his face. Why was he even thinking that? He knew exactly what had gone wrong. The little guy had nearly finished the entire bottle without burping once. And according to what he'd read on the internet—that wasn't good.

He tried to switch off from the screaming. Tried to focus his mind elsewhere. Who would leave a baby outside in the cold?

The thought had been preying on his mind since the second Carrie had found the baby. Sure, he'd done the cop thing and made a half-hearted attempt to look for the mother—to see if someone was in trouble out there.

But truth be told—he wasn't that sure he wanted to find her.

Some people just weren't fit to be parents. Fact.

He was living proof and had the scars to back up his theory.

Even twenty-five years ago social services had tried to support his mother to keep him, when the truth of the matter was they should have got him the hell out of there.

Thank goodness his grandmother had realised what the scars on his back were. The guys in the station thought they were chicken-pox scars, and he wasn't about to tell them any different. But cigarettes left a nasty permanent burn.

The expression on Carrie's face had said it all. She'd felt compassion; she'd felt pity for the person who'd left this baby behind. He felt differently. Maybe this little guy was going to get the start in life he deserved.

There was a light tap at the door, then it was shouldered open. Carrie—with a wooden crib in her hands.

She wrinkled her nose at the noise. 'What did you do?' She crossed the room and sat the crib at his feet. Had she been with Mrs Van Dyke all this time? It was the only place she could have got the crib.

He shrugged his shoulders. 'Fed him.'

She shook her head. 'He shouldn't be squealing like that. Give him here.' She held out her arms and he hesitated. What was going on? This woman had hightailed it out of here as if there were a fire licking at her heels. Now she was back as if nothing had happened?

He placed his hand protectively on the little guy's back. 'What happened, Carrie?' He didn't care how blunt it sounded. He didn't care how much help he really wanted right now. He needed her to be straight with him.

She looked him straight in the eye. But he could see it—the waver. The hesitation in her blue eyes. 'I needed a little space for five minutes. And now—I've had it. I spent a little time with Mrs Van Dyke. She's great. I wish I'd had the opportunity to speak to her before today.' She walked over to the sink and lifted one of the pacifiers out of the sterilising solution. 'Has this been in there thirty minutes?'

He glanced at the clock and nodded, watching as she put the pacifier in the baby's mouth and lifted him from his shoulder. 'Let's try something else, then.' She sat down on the sofa and laid the baby across her lap, face down, gently rubbing his back.

Dan looked at the crib and shook his head. 'I hadn't even thought about where he was going to sleep.'

Carrie smiled. The kind of smile that changed the whole expression on her face. There it was. That little glimpse again of who she could be if she let herself.

'Neither did I. I asked Mrs Van Dyke if she had any clothes and it was she who suggested the crib.' She peered over at him as she continued to rub the baby's back. 'We don't have a mattress, though. Do you have something we could put inside?'

Dan tried to rack his brain. 'What about

those new towels? We used one earlier, but I have plenty left. I could fold some of them to make a mattress for the crib.'

'That sounds perfect. I don't have a lot of clothes. A few cardigans, some embroidered vests and some socks. She also gave me a beautiful crocheted blanket. It looks brand new.'

The baby had stopped crying. Dan turned his head just in time to see a little pull up of the legs and to hear the loudest burp known to man.

'There we go. Is that better, little guy?' Carrie had turned him over and lifted him up again, staring him in the face. She put him back on her shoulder and kept gently rubbing his back. Her tongue ran along her lips. 'I remember somebody mentioning that trapped wind makes a baby cranky.'

Dan let out a snort. 'Cranky? You call that cranky? You only had to listen to five minutes of it.'

She bit her lip. 'Yes, I know. Sorry.' He could see her take a deep breath. 'I find this difficult, Dan. And I'm not sure I'll be much help.' She stood up and walked over to the window with the baby on her shoulder. 'I can't help feeling really sorry for whoever is out there. Why didn't they think they could take care of their baby? I wish I could help them.'

There it was again. The sympathy vote. The thing he just couldn't understand.

'Maybe they don't want our help. Maybe they just weren't designed to be a parent. There's a good chance they didn't have any prenatal care for the baby. Why on earth would they leave a baby on a doorstep? They didn't even ring the doorbell! This little guy could have frozen out there—he wasn't properly dressed or even fed. No diaper. He could have died during delivery. This isn't a person who wants a baby, Carrie. This is a person who has no sense of duty or responsibility.'

She spun around. 'You don't know that, Dan. You don't know anything. This could be an underage girl's baby. She might have been terrified to tell anyone she was pregnant—afraid of the repercussions. What if she was abused? What if she lives with her abuser? Have you thought of that?'

He was trying not to get mad. He was trying not to shout. He took a long, slow breath, his eyes lifting to meet hers. 'It could also be the baby of someone who wasn't interested in prenatal care. Someone who wasn't interested in making sure their baby was delivered safely. Someone who doesn't really care what happens to their baby.'

There was a tremble in her voice. 'You don't

know that, Dan.' She looked down at the baby. 'You don't know anything. I just can't imagine what would make someone dump their baby on a doorstep. But I've got to believe they were desperate and wanted their baby to get help.' Her hand stroked the baby's head. 'A baby is a precious gift. I don't know any mother who would give their baby up willingly.'

'Then I guess our experiences of life are different.' The words were out before he knew it. No hesitation. No regrets.

Her eyes met his. It was as if she was trying to take stock of what he'd just said. As if she was trying to see inside his head.

He gave himself a shake and walked over next to her. 'I agree with you, Carrie. I think babies are precious and they should be treated with respect. So I think we should do something.' He lifted his finger and touched the baby's cheek.

'What?'

'I think we should give our baby a name.'

CHAPTER FIVE

SHE LOOKED STUNNED.

As if he'd just suggested packing up the car and heading off into the sunset with a baby in tow.

'What? We can't keep calling him "the little guy". You know what happens with abandoned babies. At some point somebody, somewhere gives them a name.'

'But we don't have any right. This isn't our baby.' She gave a little shake as if the thought was too alarming.

'Actually, right now, he is our baby. And might continue to be so for the next few days. We have to call him something in the meantime. Calling him "baby", "him" or "it", it's just not right. You know it isn't.'

She'd started pacing now. Walking about the apartment. Her eyes refusing to meet with his. 'Well, what's your suggestion, genius? Do you want to call him Dan?'

She was mocking him. For some reason, she was uncomfortable with this.

'I don't want to call him Dan. That will just get confusing. I'm trying to make this *less* confusing, not more.' He looked at her again; her pacing was slowing. 'What kind of names do you like?'

'I'm not naming him.' The words snapped out of her mouth.

'Why not?'

'Because he's not my baby.'

He shook his head. 'We know this. That's not the point. Let's find something we can agree on. Do you like crazy names like Moonwind or Shooting Star? Do you like modern names, celebrity names or something more traditional?'

Her chin was on the floor. 'Moonwind? Shooting Star? You've got to be kidding?'

He shook his head and rolled his eyes. 'You forget. I'm a cop in New York. I've heard everything.'

'Wow.' She sat back down on the sofa and picked up the bottle of milk. 'I'm going to try and give him a little more of this.' She watched as his mouth closed around the teat and he started to suck. 'I guess I like more traditional names,' she finally said.

'Plain? Like John or Joe or Bob?'

'No. They are too plain. Something proud.

Something that makes you sit up and take notice.'

'I thought you'd ruled out Moonwind?'

There was a sparkle in her eyes as she turned to him. 'How about really traditional? How about something biblical?'

'Now you're really testing me. I'll need to think back to my Sunday school days.'

'Then you do that. How about Joseph? Or Isaac, or Jeremiah?'

He grabbed the first names that sprang into his mind. 'Noah, or David, or Goliath?' he countered. He wanted to make her smile again. And it worked. She was sitting up a little straighter. Trying to beat him at this game.

He could see her start to rack her brains. 'Peter, Paul or Matthew?'

'Adam, Moses or Joshua?'

There was silence for a few seconds as they both concentrated hard.

'Abraham.'

'Abraham.'

Their voices intermingled. And a smile appeared across both their faces.

Carrie stared down at the baby. 'Abraham,' she whispered. 'Now there's a proud name. What do you think of that one?'

He sat down next to her. 'Abraham, I like it.

Also the name of one of our finest presidents. It's perfect.'

'It does seem perfect.' She was staring down at the little face as he sucked at the bottle. She nodded. 'You're right. We do need to give him a name—even if it's temporary. What a pity his mum didn't leave a note with what she'd called him.' There was a wistfulness in her voice. The sympathy vote that grated on him.

'Might have been better if she'd actually left some clothes. Or some diapers. Or anything at all to show us she cared about her son.'

Carrie gave the tiniest shake of her head as she eased the bottle out of Abraham's mouth, then sat him upright, putting her hand under his chin to support his head while she rubbed his back. 'Let's see if we can get a burp out of you this time.'

She turned to face him. 'You're really hard on people, Dan. And I find it really strange. You didn't hesitate to try and help this baby. You weren't even too upset when Shana told you that you'd need to keep him a while. We have no idea what's happened here. Can you at least try to give his mother the benefit of the doubt?'

'No.'

Just like that. Blunt and to the point.

Abraham arched his back and let out a big

burp. 'Good boy.' His head started to sag. 'He's tired. Maybe we should put him down to sleep.'

Dan nodded and started folding up the towels he'd pulled from his cupboard, forming a makeshift kind of mattress in the crib. 'What do you think?'

'Perfect.' She had to put him down. She had to put him down now. She was starting to feel a little overwhelmed again. A baby cuddling into the nape of her neck and giving little sighs of comfort was making a whole host of emotions wash over her. None that she wanted to share.

She adjusted Abraham and laid him down in the crib, covering him with the hand-knitted shawl, and held her breath, waiting to see if he would stir.

It took her a few seconds to realise Dan was holding his breath right next to her.

But Abraham was out cold. His first feed had been a success.

'Darn it. Do you think we should have changed his nappy again?'

Dan raised his eyebrows. 'I think if you touch Abraham right now and wake him up I will kill you.'

She gave a little laugh. 'It's kind of strange, isn't it? Standing here waiting to see if he'll wake up again?'

Dan straightened his back. 'What time is

it?' He looked over at the kitchen clock. 'Ten-thirty? Wow. No wonder I'm starved. I haven't eaten dinner. What about you? Are you hungry, Carrie?'

She shook her head. 'Maybe I should go.'

'You are joking, right?'

She shook her head firmly. All of a sudden there wasn't a baby as a barrier between the two of them.

All of sudden there wasn't a whole lot of space between them. And it was as if a little switch had been flicked.

Everything about Dan was making her feel self-conscious. How was her hair? Was her make-up still in place?

She'd spent the past few months going around in a fog. It had never once crossed her mind how she looked to the opposite sex.

But there was something about Dan. Something about being in close proximity to him that was making her feel uncomfortable. She didn't want to have to think about all those kinds of feelings resurrecting themselves. Not when she knew where they could eventually lead.

Now, she was fixating on his straight white teeth, the little lines of fatigue around his eyes and the sincerity in his face.

Then he snapped her out of it by giving her

a cheeky wink and folding his arms across his chest. 'If I have to arrest you, I will.'

She jolted out of her daze. 'Arrest me?'

He smiled. 'To keep you here. To force you to help me look after Abraham overnight. What do I know about a newborn baby?'

'And what do I know?' She felt the rage surge inside her along with something else she couldn't quite work out. 'Because I'm a woman you think I should know about babies?'

'No.' His words were firm and strangely calming. They must have taught him that in cop school. How to calm a raging bull. 'I think you're another human being and two heads are better than one.'

It sounded logical. It sounded sensible. And it made all the chauvinistic arguments that had leaped into her head feel pathetic.

She didn't want to spend the night with a new baby. How on earth would she cope? It could end up bringing back a whole host of memories she didn't know how to deal with.

Then there was Dan. With his short dark hair and big brown eyes that made her skin itch. No, that made her skin *tingle*.

Every now and then he flirted with her, as if it was his natural demeanour. Flirting with women was obviously second nature to a guy like him. But it wasn't second nature for her.

And she just didn't have the defences for it yet. She didn't want to be drawn in by his twinkling eyes and cheeky grins. She would look like some hapless teenager around him. This was feeling more awkward by the minute.

Carrie walked back over to the window, sneaking a look at Abraham on the way past.

'How long do you think he'll sleep?'

She shook her head. 'Yet another thing I'll need to look up. Isn't it usually around four hours for new babies?'

Dan glanced at the clock. 'So we've got until two-thirty.' He smiled. 'Do you want the night shift or shall I?'

Carrie hesitated. 'I'm not sure about this, Dan. I told you I've got no experience with babies. How am I supposed to know if something is wrong or not? I can't read everything you're supposed to know about babies in a few hours. What if we do something we shouldn't?'

He lifted his hands. 'We can only do our best. And anyway, look at you earlier—you were a natural.'

The words sent a chill down her spine. She knew he didn't mean for that to happen—he probably meant the words as a compliment. But her mind and body just couldn't react that way.

She was trying to partition this whole experience in her head. Put it inside a little box that could be safely stowed away somewhere.

Somewhere safe.

This was hard. And the reality was, it was only going to get harder. She'd felt herself waver a few moments before when Abraham had snuggled into her neck and she'd caught that distinctive baby scent in her nostrils.

She knew it was time to back off. To give herself a little space. And if she could keep doing that she might actually survive this experience.

And let's face it. Dan was hardly a strain on the eyes.

Why hadn't they ever spoken before? Had she really seemed so unapproachable? So caught up in her own world?

She watched as he looked in his cupboards, trying to find something to eat. Eventually he pulled some glasses and a bottle of soda from the cupboard. She could see the taut muscles across his back through his thin T-shirt. She tried not to stare at the outline of his behind in the well-worn jeans.

Her eyes automatically went downwards. Would he look at her the same way? Maybe she should have given some more thought to what she was wearing.

'I see you've finally got some clothes on.'

She gave a little smile as she walked over and sat down at the table. 'I didn't really have time to think earlier. I don't often roam around strange men's apartments in my nightclothes.'

'You don't?' He had a gleam in his eyes. He was trying to lighten the mood. Ease the stress they were both under. 'Is your apartment cold upstairs? You were bundled up like you live in an igloo.'

She took a sip of the soda he'd just poured for her. 'No. It was comfort clothes. I was freezing when I got in—I ruined my suede boots walking in that mucky slush. My raincoat was covered in muddy splatters and all I could think about was getting inside, heating up and eating myself silly.'

He tilted his head as he sat down. In this dim light in the kitchen he had really dark brown eyes. Comforting kind of eyes. The kind you could lose yourself in.

'And what does eating yourself silly involve?'

She shrugged. 'Chocolate. In all varieties. Macaroni cheese. Grilled bagels with melted cheese. Porridge. Pancakes.' She pointed towards the ceiling. 'I bought some stuff at Mr Meltzer's before I came home. I was worried I'd be stuck inside for a few days with no comfort foods.' She gave him a grin and shook her head. 'Believe me, that would *not* be pretty.'

He eyed her closely, the smell of pizza starting to fill the apartment. 'And would you be willing to share some of your stash?'

Her smile widened. The atmosphere was changing between them. They were going from frantic neighbours to something else entirely. Were they flirting here? Was that what was happening? It had been so long for Carrie she wasn't sure she remembered how.

She rested her elbows on the table, sitting her head in her hands. 'Oh, I don't know about sharing. I might be willing to trade.'

'Aha, a wolf in sheep's clothing.'

'What does that mean?'

The gleam wasn't disappearing; in fact, if it was possible, it was getting naughtier. 'You come down here with your innocent smiles, woolly socks and grandma pyjamas—not forgetting an abandoned baby—with your tales of a huge pirate haul of comfort foods upstairs, and now you're trying to hold me to ransom.' He leaned back in his chair and tapped the surface of the table. 'You're not really a grandma-pyjamas girl, are you? That was all just a ruse—you're really a sexy negligee kind of girl.' He lifted his hand and tapped his chin. 'The question is, what colour?'

She could feel her cheeks start to pink up. She hadn't been imagining it. He was flirting with her. And the thing that amazed her—or terrified her—was she wanted to flirt right back. Could she trade her bagels for a kiss?

Wow. That thought made the blood rush into her cheeks. 'What's wrong with grandma pyjamas? They hide a multitude of sins.'

He didn't hesitate. 'You don't have any sins to hide.'

She felt her breath stall. She couldn't breathe in. She definitely couldn't breathe out. She was stuck in that no man's land. He'd said it so quickly. He didn't even have to think about it twice.

What did that mean?

She made a vague attempt to laugh it off—feeling like a nervous teenager instead of a capable twenty-seven-year-old woman. 'You're a man. You really have no knowledge of water-filled bras or hold-your-gut-in underwear.'

He leaned across the table towards her. A cheeky smile across his face. 'And you have no need for either.'

He stayed there. Inches away from her face. Letting her see the tiny, fine laughter lines around his eyes and the smattering of freckles across his cheeks.

Up close and personal Daniel Cooper looked good enough to eat.

And then there was the smell. His cologne.

It was affecting her senses. Everything seemed heightened.

Her skin prickled, her hairs standing upright. Her mouth felt dry, her tongue running across her lips.

She couldn't take her eyes off his mouth. Or maybe it was his brown eyes. The kind you could melt into. Both were distracting her. Both were making entirely inappropriate thoughts about a man she hardly knew invade her brain and send a warm feeling to her stomach.

A feeling she hadn't felt since…

It was like a bucket of cold water being tipped over her head. That, and the awareness of the little contented noises from the crib off to the side.

That was why she was here.

Not for any other reason. Dan wasn't interested in her. Not really. He just didn't want to be stuck with some strange baby on his own. He'd made that perfectly clear.

The rest?

She hardly knew the guy, and with handsome looks and a job like his? He probably had women eating out of the palm of his hand.

The thought made her pull back in her chair, her sudden movement causing him to blink and a wrinkle to appear on his brow.

She fixed her eyes on the table. They were safe there.

'Don't you have a friend you can call to help you with Abraham overnight? I'm sure you must have plenty of female friends who'd be willing to give you a hand.'

'What does that mean?'

She shrugged, trying to look complacent. Trying to pretend she hadn't just almost asked him out loud if he had a girlfriend. 'It means there must be someone other than me who can give you a hand.'

He shook his head. 'All the female cops I know are currently run off their feet on duty. My friends who are married all stay too far away to get here and help.' He rolled his eyes. 'And the past few female companions I've had—I wouldn't let within fifty feet of this little guy.'

She almost choked on her soda. 'Then maybe you should be more selective with your female friends.' It was meant to sound playful, but it came out like a chastisement. All because her insides were wound up so tightly.

He shrugged his shoulders. 'Maybe I should.'

It was left hanging in the air between them.

She had no idea what to make of that. She shifted uncomfortably in the chair. 'You mean there's absolutely no one you can ask to help you out?'

'Just you.'

'Dan…' She looked out at the falling snow. If it were even possible, it seemed to be falling even heavier.

She looked around the apartment and threw her hands in the air. 'I don't like this, Dan. I don't know you and you don't know me. It doesn't matter that you're a cop and one of the "good guys".' She put her fingers in the air and made the sign. 'Baby or no baby, I can't stay in an apartment with some strange guy. I'm just not comfortable.'

He leaned back in his chair, watching her with those intense brown eyes.

'What if I promise not to come near you at night? You can sleep in my room and I'll sleep on the sofa. We can move the crib during the night. That way—you'll still have some privacy but we'll both know the other is there if we need a hand.'

Her. In a room by herself with Abraham in a crib. She was going to throw up right there and then.

And then Dan did something. He reached across the table and took her hand. 'I need help, Carrie. I need you. Don't say you can't do it.'

A lump a mile wide appeared in her throat.

He was leaning towards her in the dim light. Her eyes fixated on his lips. What was wrong with her? And what was wrong with her emotions?

Everything about her wanted to run right now.

But her ethics and her goodwill were making her stay. She couldn't abandon Abraham right now. His own mother had already done that.

She had been the one to find him. She should be the one responsible for him.

'I feel really awkward about all this, Dan.' She sighed.

'Then let's see if we can make you feel un-awkward.'

'Is that even a word?'

'It is now.' He put his head in his hands. 'So, Carrie McKenzie, what's your favourite movie?'

'What?' It was so not what she was expecting. She was expecting him to pry. To ask why she'd reacted like that. To ask what had been wrong with her this whole evening.

The question was totally random and took her by surprise. It took a few seconds for her brain to think of an appropriate response. 'If it's adults' it's *Dirty Dancing*. If it's kids' then definitely *Toy Story*. What kind of a question is that anyway?'

'A getting-to-know-you question,' he said as he took a sip of his soda. Just like that. So matter-of-fact. Boy, this guy didn't mess around. He raised his eyebrows at her. 'What? You've never been on a date and done the getting-to-know-you questions before?'

She opened her mouth to react, to ask what he meant, then stopped herself dead. He was being casual. He was being cool. And anything she would say right now would be distinctly *uncool*.

One moment she'd been staring into his eyes wondering what it would be like to kiss him— next they were having a first-date kind of conversation.

She took a deep breath. 'It's been a while,' she said quietly. 'I guess I'm out of practice.'

'How long?'

His question was fired back straight away. She could tell a lie here and try and pretend to be blasé. But it just didn't suit her. 'About seven years.' She lifted her head and looked him straight in the eye. She'd had to think about that. Had it really been that long? She'd dated Mark for five years before she was pregnant with Ruby, and it had been more than a year since then. To Dan's credit he didn't even blink, no smart remarks, no more questions. It was as if he just filed the information away for use at a later date.

She shouldn't have said anything. It was time to move things back to the original question. Get off this subject completely. 'You do realise I had to leave out the musicals—for obvious reasons.'

The eyebrows lifted even further. 'What obvious reasons?'

She shrugged. 'I couldn't possibly count them. I'll have you know I know the words to every song of every musical ever made.' She gave him a cheeky wink. 'And some of the dance moves.'

He leaned across the table towards her. 'The thing that scares me about that is—I believe you.' He kept his eyes fixed on hers. 'I might ask to see some of those dance moves.'

She gulped. Colour was rushing to her cheeks. She'd been premature with that wink. Trying to appear sassier and way cooler than she actually was. Maybe not her best idea. Especially when she could almost feel the heat radiating from him. It was time to get this back to safer territory. 'What about you?' That was easy. That kept everything on an even keel.

'Definitely *The Great Escape,* with Steve McQueen on the motorbike. Nothing can beat that.'

She nodded. She'd watched the movie a hundred times—knew some of the lines by heart. 'And a kids' movie?'

He had the good grace to look a little bashful. 'You might be surprised. But I love *Finding Nemo*. I love Marlin and Dory. It's one of those movies that you turn the TV on, walk past and find yourself sucked in for two hours. Just like that.' He snapped his fingers.

She couldn't help the smile that was plastered on her face. 'I wouldn't have taken you for a *Finding Nemo* kind of guy.'

He took another sip of soda. 'See? There's lots you don't know about me. And vice versa. Are you feeling a little less awkward now.'

She let out a little laugh. 'Just because I know what films you like doesn't mean I feel comfortable about staying in your apartment overnight.'

He nodded slowly. 'So, what brought you to New York, then, Carrie? I know your business owns the apartment upstairs, but why you? Why now?'

There it was. The killer question—sneaked on in there when her defences were down. She should have seen this coming.

How could she answer that? How could she answer any of that without giving herself away?

She picked up her glass and walked over to the sink. 'I'll do the dishes.' She started running the hot water and putting some washing-up liquid into the basin. 'Seems only fair.'

'But what if we're not finished yet?'

He knew. He knew exactly what she was doing. Distraction. Avoidance.

She jumped. His voice was just at her shoulder. His warm breath next to her ear. 'What do you mean?' Darn it. Her voice was wavering. He would have heard it. He would know the effect he was having on her.

So much for acting cool.

He slid his glass in next to hers, his arms on either side of her body, capturing her between them.

She could feel him up against her. One part of her wanted to relax. To let herself relax against him as if this was the most natural thing in the world.

But her frantically beating heart wouldn't let her. And her oxygen-deprived brain wasn't playing ball, either.

She watched the bubbles form in the warm water. Letting them come halfway up her arms.

And what did he mean anyhow?

His hands slid into the basin next to hers. His head coming forward and almost resting on her shoulder. 'I mean, what if we're not finished with this conversation? What if I think you just avoided my question and I want to know why?' His hands were over hers now and her breath hitched in her chest. 'What if I want to get to know you a little better, Carrie McKenzie? Despite our unusual meeting—and despite our chaperone.'

He lifted up a finger and held it in the air. It was covered in bubbles, with the light reflecting off them revealing a rainbow of colours. She couldn't speak. She didn't know what to say—how to respond. Plus she was mesmerised by the bubbles popping one by one. He gave a little laugh, moved his finger and smudged the bubbles on her nose.

She breathed in quickly in surprise, inhaling half the bubbles, leading to a coughing fit. All she could hear was Dan's hearty laughter as she half choked to death, doubled over, then she felt his hand on her back, sharply at first, giving a few knocks to ease her choking, then soothing, rubbing her back while she caught her breath again.

She finally stood upright, his hand still positioned on her back, damp from being in the sink. His other hand fell naturally to her hip.

She turned her head to look at him. 'What was that for?'

'Fun.' He was grinning at her. Showing off his perfect teeth and American good-boy looks.

It was like temptation all in one package.

She bit her lip. 'You've got me all wet.' She squirmed as she pulled her T-shirt from her back. Then cringed at her words. No! She hadn't really said that out loud, had she? She could feel the blood rush to her cheeks. *Please don't let him take anything from that.*

But he just gave her that sexy smile again. 'We can't have that. Do you want something else to wear?' He walked towards one of the doors in the apartment—most likely his bedroom. 'I'm sure I've something in here for you.'

It was blatant. It was obvious. He was full of it.

She folded her arms across her chest. She should be insulted, but the truth was she wasn't really. She was a tiny bit flattered.

She shook her head. 'You were the college playboy, weren't you?'

He leaned against the doorjamb. 'What if I was?'

'Then you should be used to women thinking you're too big for your boots.'

The tension in the air was killing her. If this were a movie she would just walk over, wink and lead him into the bedroom.

He sighed and looked skyward. 'I love it when you talk dirty to me. It's the accent. It's killing me. Every time you talk I just—'

There was a little grunt from the corner of

the room and they both leaped about a foot in the air.

Every other thought was pushed out of the window.

In the blink of an eye they were both at the side of the crib, leaning overtop the still-sleeping baby.

'Did that mean something?' asked Dan.

'How am I supposed to know?' she whispered back.

She watched Abraham's little chest rise and fall, rise and fall. It was soothing. It was calming.

'Did we decide on who was doing the night shift?'

She wanted to say no. She wanted to say she couldn't do it and retreat back upstairs to the safety of her silent apartment.

She wanted to put the random flirtations out of her head.

But there was so much churning around in her mind.

This baby. Abraham.

He didn't have a mother to comfort him right now. Being around him was hard. Being around him was torture.

But what if this was something she had to do? What if this was something she had to get past?

Sure, she'd grieved for her daughter. She'd wept a bucketload of tears and spent weeks thinking 'what if?' She'd watched her relationship slowly but surely disintegrate around her and Mark. They'd both known it was inevitable, but that hadn't made the parting any easier.

So she'd been bereft. She'd been empty.

But had she allowed herself to heal?

And Dan wasn't anything like Mark. Mark hadn't walked from their relationship—he'd practically run.

And here was Dan stepping in, and taking responsibility—albeit temporarily—for an unknown baby on their doorstep. Maybe for five minutes she should stop judging all men by Mark's standard. Maybe she should take a little time to get to know someone like Dan. Someone who might restore her faith in humanity again.

And did she even know how to do that?

She straightened up, pushing her hands into her back and cricking her spine. Dan was at her back again. 'Carrie, are you okay? Is there something you want to tell me?'

This was it. This was her opportunity to tell him why she was acting so strangely around him and this baby. This was a chance for her to be honest.

This was a chance to clear the air between them.

But she was torn. There was a buzz between them.

They were both feeling it. She liked the flirtation. It made her feel good. It made her feel normal again. Even though there was nothing about this situation that was normal.

She barely knew Dan, but just being in his company made her feel safe. The way he'd reacted to the abandoned baby. The way he'd immediately gone out into the snowstorm to look for the mother, even if he really didn't want to. The way he wasn't afraid to roll up his sleeves and help take care of a baby, even with no experience.

But what would happen right now if she told him?

She could almost get out a huge crystal ball and predict it. The moment she said the words, *'I had a stillbirth last year. My daughter died,'* it would kill anything between them stone dead. It would destroy this buzz in the air.

It would destroy the first feel-good feelings she'd felt in over a year.

So, no matter how hard this was, and for what were totally selfish reasons, she wanted to stay. She might feel a sense of duty, a sense of responsibility towards Abraham, but that wasn't all she was feeling.

And right now she wanted to do something for herself.

For Carric.

Was that really so selfish?

She took a deep breath and turned around to face him.

It would be so easy. It would be so easy to lean forward just a little and see what might happen.

To see if this buzz in the air could amount to anything.

To hold her breath and see if he was sensing what she was feeling—or to see that it had been *so* long that her reactions were completely off. Completely wrong.

He reached up and touched her cheek. 'Carrie?'

She swallowed, biting back the words she really wanted to say and containing the actions she really wanted to take.

She didn't want anything to destroy that tiny little buzz that was currently in her stomach. It felt precious to her. As if it was finally the start of something new.

'How about I take the first shift? I'll sleep on the sofa next to the crib and do the first feed and change at night. You can take over after that.'

She kept her voice steady and her words firm. She could see something flicker behind his eyes. The questions that he really wanted to ask. He nodded and gave her a little smile.

'Welcome to your first night shift, Carrie McKenzie.'

She watched his retreating back as she sat down on the sofa.

Was she wrong about all this?

Only time, and a whole heap of snow, would tell.

CHAPTER SIX

CARRIE STRETCHED ON the sofa and groaned. The early morning sun was trying to creep through the blinds. It was brighter than normal, which probably meant it was reflecting off the newly laid white snow. All thoughts of everything returning to normal today vanished in the drop of a snowflake.

There was no getting away from it—Baby Abraham was hard work.

She hadn't had time last night to feel sorry for herself and neither had Dan—because Abraham had screamed for three hours solid. She certainly hadn't had time for any romantic dreams. It seemed neither of them had the knack for feeding and burping a new baby.

'Carrie?' Dan came stumbling through the doorway, bleary-eyed, his hair all rumpled and his low-slung jeans skimming his hips.

She screwed up her eyes. Bare-chested. He was bare-chested again. Did the guy always walk about like this? Her brain couldn't cope with a cute naked guy this early in the morning, especially when she was sleep-deprived.

She pointed her finger at him. 'If you wake him, I swear, Dan Cooper, I'll come over there and—'

'Cook me pancakes?'

She sighed and sagged back down onto the sofa, landing on another uncomfortable lump. 'You have the worst sofa known to man.' She twisted on her side and thumped at the lump. 'Oh, it's deceptive. It looks comfortable. When you sit down, you sink into it and think, *Wow!* But sleeping on it?' She blew her hair off her forehead. 'Not a chance!'

'Wanna take the bed tomorrow night?'

With or without you?

She pushed the wayward thought out of her head. How did parents ever go on to have more than one child? Hanky-panky must be the last thing on their minds.

She stood up and stretched. Abraham had finally quietened down around an hour ago. He was now looking all angelic, breathing steadily as if sleeping came easily to him.

'The offer of pancakes sounds good. Do you think you can cook them without waking His Lordship? Because at this rate, ancient or not,

Mrs Van Dyke's going to have to take her turn babysitting.'

Dan nodded. 'Right there with you, Carrie. For some reason I thought this would be a breeze. You've no idea how many times I nearly picked up the phone to call Shana last night and beg her to come and pick him up.'

Carrie leaned against the door, giving him her sternest stare. 'Well, maybe you need to think about that a little more.'

'What do you mean?'

'You've been pretty down on Abraham's mum. We're presuming he was just born. But what if he's actually a few days old? Maybe she was struggling to cope. Maybe she's young—or old—and didn't have any help. Maybe she's sick.'

The dark cloud quickly descended over Dan's face again. 'Stop it, Carrie. Stop trying to make excuses for her. And if Abraham's not newly born, then where were his diapers? Where were his clothes? And no matter how hard she was finding it to cope—is that really a good enough reason to dump a baby on a freezing doorstep?'

She shrugged her shoulders. 'I'm just throwing it out there, Dan. I'm not trying to make excuses for anyone. What I am going to do is take a shower and change my clothes.' She headed over to the door. 'I'll be back in ten minutes and I expect my breakfast to be waiting.' She gave him a wink.

He lifted his eyebrows. 'Hmm, getting all feisty now, are we? I think I preferred you when you were all *please help me with this baby.*'

She picked up the nearest cushion and tossed it at his head. 'No, you didn't,' she said as she headed out the door.

'No. I didn't,' he breathed as he watched her head upstairs.

Carrie took a few moments to pull open her blinds and look outside.

A complete white-out with no signs of life. Not a single footprint on the sidewalk. Every car was covered in snow, with not a single chance of moving anywhere soon. It seemed that New York City would remain at a standstill for another day.

For a moment she wished she were in the middle of Central Park. Maybe standing at Belvedere Castle and looking out over the Great Lawn, or standing on Bow Bridge watching the frozen lake. It would be gorgeous there right now.

She didn't care that it was closed because of the snowfall. She didn't care about the potential for falling trees. All she could think about was how peaceful it would be right now—and how beautiful.

But with daydreams like this, was she just looking for another opportunity to hide away?

She tried to push the thoughts from her head. There was too much going on in there. What with virtually bare baby and bare-chested Dan, her head was spinning.

She switched on the shower and walked through to her bedroom, stripping off her clothes and pulling her dressing gown on while she waited for the water to heat.

The contents of her wardrobe seemed to mock her. A sparkly sequin T-shirt. Trying too hard. A red cardigan. Impersonating Mrs Van Dyke. A plain jumper. Frumpy.

She pulled out another set of jeans and a bright blue cap-sleeved sweater. It would have to do.

Her eyes caught sight of the silver box beneath her bed and her heart flipped over.

It was calling her. It was willing her to open it.

She couldn't help it. It was automatic. She knelt down and touched it, pulling it out from under the bed and sitting it on top of the bed in front of her.

Her precious memories, all stored in a little

box. But how could she look at them now after she'd just been holding another baby?

It almost seemed like a betrayal.

She ran the palm of her hand over the lid of the box. Just doing it made her heartbeat quicken. She could feel the threat of tears at the backs of her eyes.

She couldn't think about this now. She just couldn't.

Steam was starting to emerge from the bathroom. The shower was beckoning. She couldn't open the box. Not now. Not while she was in the middle of all this.

For the contents of that box she needed space. She needed time.

She needed the ability to cry where no one could hear. No one could interrupt.

She sucked air into her lungs. Not now. She had to be strong. She had to be focused. Her hand moved again—one last final touch of the silver box of memories—before she tore herself away and headed inside, closing the door firmly behind her.

There was a whimper in the corner. Dan's pancakes were sizzling; was the noise going to wake the baby? He sure hoped not. He didn't know if he could take another cryfest.

The television newscaster looked tired. He'd

probably been stuck inside the New York studio all night. The yellow information strip ran along the bottom of the news constantly. Telling them how much snow had fallen, how the city was stranded, all businesses were closed, food supplies couldn't get in. Nothing about how to look after a newborn baby.

It was time to do an internet search again. They must have done something wrong last night. There was no way a baby would cry like that for nothing. At least he hoped not.

He tossed the pancakes and his stomach growled loudly. He was starving and they smelled great.

A jar of raspberry jam landed on the counter next to him. She was back. And she smelled like wild flowers—even better than pancakes.

'What's that for?'

'The pancakes.'

'Jelly?' He shook his head. 'Pancakes need bacon and maple syrup. That's what a real pancake wants.'

She opened his fridge. 'Pancakes need butter and raspberry jam. It's the only way to eat them.'

He wrinkled his nose, watching as she flicked on the kettle.

'And tea. Pancakes need tea.'

He grimaced. 'You might be out of luck, then. I've only got extra-strong coffee.'

She waved a bag at him. 'Just as well I brought my own, then.'

Dan served the pancakes onto two plates and carried them over to the table, pulling some syrup from his empty cupboards and lifting the brewing coffee pot. 'I can't tempt you, then?'

Something flickered in her eyes. Something else. Something different. She gave him a hesitant smile. 'I'm an English girl. It's tea and butter and jam all the way.'

They both knew that the flirtation was continuing.

And right now he wanted to tempt her. The cop in him wanted to forget about the mountain of paperwork he'd need to complete about this baby. The cop in him wanted to forget about the investigation that would have to be carried out.

The guy in him wanted to concentrate on the woman in the lovely blue sweater sitting at his table with her jar of raspberry jam. He wanted to reach over to touch the curls that were coiling around her face, springing free from the clip that was trying to hold them back. He wanted to see if he could say something to make her cheeks flush even pinker than they currently werc. He wanted a chance to stare into those cornflower-blue eyes and ask her what she was hiding from him. What she was guarding herself from.

He lifted the maple syrup and squirted it onto his pancakes. She was concentrating on spreading butter on her pancakes smoothly and evenly with one hand while stirring her tea with the other hand.

He'd opened the blinds partly to let a little natural light into the apartment. And seeing Carrie McKenzie in the cold light of day was more than just a little shock to his system.

The girl was beautiful. From the little sprinkle of freckles over her nose to the way she wrinkled her brow when she was concentrating.

He'd felt a pull towards her last night, when he'd seen her in the dim lights of his apartment. But now he had a chance to look at her—to really look at her—and all he could think about was why on earth he hadn't noticed her before.

How on earth could he have stayed in an apartment building with someone so incredibly pretty and not have noticed? He could just imagine the cops at the station if they ever got wind of that.

Carrie put a teaspoon into the jam jar and spread some jam onto her pancakes. 'Are you going to watch me eat them, too?' she asked, a smile spreading across her face.

He jerked backwards in his seat. 'Sorry. I was just thinking.'

'About Abraham?'

Wow. No, Abraham was the last thing he'd been thinking about, and as if in indignation there was a squawk from the crib. Dan set down his cutlery, gave a sigh and waved his hand at her as she went to stand up. 'Stay where you are—you're still eating. I'm finished. Maybe he's hungry again. I sterilised the bottles so we should be fine.'

It was amazing how quickly you could learn to make a baby bottle. A few minutes later he lifted Abraham from the crib and settled him onto his shoulder for a bit.

'Carrie? Does he look okay to you? What do you think about his colour?'

She set down her mug of tea and walked over. 'It's kind of hard to tell.' She shrugged her shoulders. 'We don't really know anything about the ethnicity of his parents, so I'm not entirely sure what normal will look like for him.'

She walked over to the window and pulled the blinds up completely. 'Bring him over here so I can get a better look at him.'

Dan carried him over and they stood for a few seconds looking at him in the daylight. 'He looks a tiny bit yellow, don't you think?'

She nodded. 'Jaundice. Isn't it supposed to be quite common in newborns?'

He gave her that smile again. The why-are-you-asking-me-something-I-couldn't-possibly-know smile.

They both glanced at the computer. Carrie took a few seconds to punch in the words and then—nothing.

She turned towards him. 'Looks like your internet has just died.'

'Really? It's usually really reliable. Must be the weather.'

She stared out the window. 'It must be something to do with the snow. I hope the power supply doesn't get hokey. That sometimes happens in storms back home.'

He looked at her with an amused expression on his face. 'Hokey?'

She raised her eyebrows. 'What? It's a word.'

'Really? Where?'

She gave him a sarcastic smile. 'I'd look it up for you online but your internet is down.'

'Ha-ha. Seriously—what are we going to do about Abraham? Do you think it's dangerous? I mean, he's drinking okay and—' he wrinkled his nose '—he certainly knows how to poo.'

She raised her eyebrows at him. 'Really? Again? Then maybe you should phone a friend. It's a bit like the blind leading the blind here. I guess you'll need to phone Shana. There really isn't anyone else we can ask.'

He gave her a smile as he walked over to put Abraham on the dark towel to change him. He could only imagine the chaos going on at Angel's Children's Hospital right now. Last thing he wanted to do was add to Shana's headache. But he wanted to make sure that Abraham was safe in his care. Screamer or not, he wanted to do the best he could for this baby.

'Do you think this is how all new parents feel? As if they don't know anything at all?'

Carrie turned her back and walked over to the countertop, picking up her mug of tea. Trying to find the words that would counteract the tight feeling in her chest. She was trying so hard. So hard not to let these things creep up on her. Then—out of the blue—some random comment would just cut her in two.

She set her mouth in a straight line. 'Most new parents would have a whole host of textbooks or family to ask—we don't.'

He pulled his mobile from his pocket. 'I guess I'll phone Shana, then.' He dialled the number and waited for Shana to be paged, pressing the button to put her on speakerphone as he wrestled with Abraham's nappy.

'What?'

Not good. She sounded snarky. 'Shana, it's Dan.'

'Is the baby okay?' Straight to the point as usual. Did she ever stop—just for a second?

He took a deep breath. 'We're not sure. Abraham looks kinda yellow. Carrie thinks he might be jaundiced.'

'Who is Abraham?'

'The baby. Who did you think I was asking about?'

'Oh, so you've given him a name. Abraham—I like it.'

'I'm glad I've got your approval. What about his colour?'

'More common in breastfed babies—but not unusual. It could be jaundice.' It was clear she was thinking out loud. 'Could be serious if it's appeared within twenty-four hours of birth—but then we don't know that, do we?'

'So what do we do now?'

'Ideally, I'd like to check him over and draw some blood.'

'Well, that's not gonna happen any time soon. What should we do in the meantime?'

'Monitor him—I mean, watch him. Make sure he feeds regularly and he's not too sleepy. Don't be afraid to wake him up to feed him. Let him get some natural light onto his skin. Put his crib next to the window and keep a close eye on his colour. If you think it's getting worse—or he has any other symptoms—phone me, straight away. Check the whites of his eyes. If they start to turn yellow you need to call me.'

Dan couldn't help it. He lifted a sleepy eyelid immediately, much to the disgust of Abraham, who squealed loudly at being disturbed.

Shana let out a laugh at the other end of the phone. 'If he's that annoyed, he's doing okay. But let me know if you're concerned.' She ended the call abruptly—probably a thousand other things to do.

Dan stared at the receiver in his hand. 'She never even told me if she contacted social services,' he murmured.

'Probably too busy.' He jumped at the quiet voice in his ear. He should have realised she'd stepped closer to him. The wave of wild flowers seemed like her trademark scent.

He held his breath. Did she realise she was standing so close? Was there something, somewhere that kept pulling them closer together? Because it sure felt like it.

Her gaze dropped to the floor and he was sorry, because he liked when she was so close he could see the other little flecks of colour in her cornflower-blue eyes. Tiny little fragments of green that you could only see up close. She tugged at the bottom of her sweater, obviously feeling a little self-conscious.

'I heard a little of that,' she said. 'Shall I move his crib over to the window?'

He nodded and she moved swiftly, pulling all the blinds up completely and drowning the room in the reflected brilliant white light from outside. He flinched, his hand on Abraham's back. 'Wow. Well, if that can't beat a bit of jaundice I don't know what will.'

She turned around and shot him a killer smile.

His reactions were automatic. Abraham was put down in the brightly lit crib and Dan found himself standing right at her side.

He was obviously going stir-crazy. Being trapped in his apartment with a beautiful lady was playing havoc with his senses. He was going to have to try and find some other way to distract himself.

All his usual self-control was flying out the window around Carrie McKenzie and he had no idea why.

She was hiding something from him. And who could blame her? They hardly knew each other. He couldn't expect her to tell him her every dark secret.

But Dan's instincts were good. Probably due to his experiences as a child. Experiences that had affected his ability to form real, trusting relationships with women.

So why was it that the first time he ever really wanted to get to know someone, he picked the one woman who was clearly hiding something? Was he crazy?

He had to do something—anything—to distract himself from all this. 'Any plans today, Carrie?'

She folded her arms across her chest. 'Apart from strapping on my jet pack to fly across New York, get to work, put in a ten-hour day, find some groceries and clothes for a stranded baby, no, nothing at all.' She was shaking her head, staring out at the five-foot-deep snow. She was obviously as stir-crazy as he was.

He waved his pink cast at her. 'Well, I'm going to go swimming. Then I'm going to strap on my skis—can't waste good snow like this— and finally I'm going to ship Shana over here to check out Abraham and make sure he's okay.' He gave her a little smile. 'And if she could bring some beers, sodas and a fresh pizza, that would be great.'

Carrie leaned against the window and sighed. 'What are we going to do all day?'

'If we can't play our imaginary games?'

Carrie counted off on her fingers. 'We could have a soapathon. You know, watch all the soaps that you haven't for years. Watch them all day.' Her brow wrinkled. 'I don't really know the names of any of the soaps in America. Are they any good?'

He shook his head. 'Next idea.'

She looked around. 'We could reorganise. Everyone needs a spring clean. It could be the perfect time.'

'Get your hands off my stuff, McKenzie,' he growled at her. 'Anyway, haven't you already realised there's nothing in my cupboards to re-organise?'

She laughed. 'Okay. I didn't think you'd go for that one.

'Do you have games? Board games? I could challenge you.' She could obviously see him racking his brain. 'Chess?' She was getting desperate.

'I might have some board games. But they will be years old. Some are probably originals.'

He walked over to a cupboard and went down on his hands and knees, crawling right inside. She heard some groans as some sports-kit bags, rackets and balls shot past her ankles. 'Need some help in there?'

There was a little cloud of dust followed by a coughing fit and Dan crawled out with a pile of games in his hands. He held them out towards her. 'How about these?'

She carried them over to the table. 'Wow. You were right—some of these are originals.' And even better than being originals, they all showed visible signs of wear and tear. It was obvious that these games had been used and loved at some point in their history. 'I think these would be perfect.'

He appeared at her side, a big smudge across his cheek. 'What does the winner get?'

She couldn't help it. Her fingers reached up to wipe the smudge from his cheek. He froze, then caught her hand in his before she could pull it away. 'What does the winner of this games tournament get?'

His words were quiet this time, the jokey aspect removed, and she could sense the feeling hanging in the air between them.

A whole variety of answers sprang to mind; some of them would make her hair curl and save her hours at the hairdressers.

Then a safe option shot into her mind. 'Can you bake?'

'What?' He looked stunned. He'd obviously had something else in mind.

'I said can you bake?'

'I suppose so. My grandmother baked all the time. But it's been years since I've tried anything like that. Anyhow, you've seen my cupboards. Old Mother Hubbard had nothing on me. I don't have any ingredients.'

'But I do. There it's settled. The loser has to make the winner a cake. Just what we need on a day like this.'

'You'd trust me to make you a cake?'

'I love cake. I'd trust anyone to make me a cake.' She held out her hand. 'Do we have a deal?'

He hesitated for just a second, before his competitive edge took over. 'I'm a chocolate cake kind of guy. You better get your apron out.'

The waft of baking filled the whole apartment. It had been years since the place had smelled like this. It only made him miss his grandmother more.

Apple pie. That had been the thing she'd baked most frequently. And it was the smell he most associated with his grandmother. Freshly baked juicy apples bubbling under the surface of the golden pie, topped with a sprinkling of sugar. Bliss.

Now the smell was a little different. The timer on the oven buzzed. He hadn't even known that his oven had a timer, let alone how to use it. But Carrie had insisted it was essential to bake the perfect cake.

Or cakes as it had turned out.

The game marathon had resulted in a dead heat.

And now his kitchen was filled with the smells of chocolate cake and carrot cake. He pulled the door open as a waft of heat flooded out from the oven. The chocolate cake that Carrie had baked for him looked spectacular. His carrot cake? Not so much. A little charred on top. But nothing that the mound of frosting she'd made him prepare couldn't hide.

He lifted both out and watched as she tipped them onto a wire rack to cool—yet another thing she'd brought down from her apartment upstairs. Along with the mixing bowls, spatulas, ingredients and cake tins. She probably had more of her possessions currently in his apartment than her own.

Baking was definitely her thing. She seemed relaxed, she seemed happy and she liked it. Even Abraham seemed to be more chilled out. Two feeds, lots of wind and no crying fits. Finally things were starting to settle.

'We need to let the cakes cool before we ice them. So let's give them a minute.' She pulled out some plates from the cupboard, then shook her head and went back to look for more.

'What's wrong with my plates'?

'Nothing.' Her voice was muffled as she

crouched in one of his kitchen cupboards. 'But cake-eating is an art form. You have to have better plates than those. Aha.' She pulled herself back out of the cupboard with something in her hand. 'These are much better.'

She stood up and put the fine bone china plates on the countertop. White with tiny red flowers painted on them. Another remnant of his grandmother. She'd used them for eating cake, too—probably why they were now hidden in the depths of his cupboards.

The lights flickered around them.

'Uh-oh,' murmured Carrie. 'That's the third time that's happened now.'

Dan walked over next to her. 'This could be a problem.'

She turned to face him. 'Why?'

'Because I don't have any candles.'

She looked at him in mock horror and held up her hands. 'You don't? What kind of emergency guy are you? Aren't you cops supposed to be prepared for anything?'

He didn't move, just kept his eyes fixed on her face. 'Not everything.' His voice was quiet, barely a whisper. There was no mistaking the alternative meaning.

She looked up at him. He was only inches from her face, inches from her lips. The lights flickered again, so he moved a little closer, his hand resting on her hip.

She didn't move. Not an inch. Her tongue came out slowly and ran along her lips, as if, without even realising it, she was preparing them for kissing.

She could feel the pull. She could feel the same draw that he felt. He wasn't wrong about this—he could tell.

It had been there all day and they had been dancing around the edges of it. But now it wasn't hiding any more. It was right there in front of them.

His fingers pressed into her hip, pulling her pelvis a little closer to his, giving her every opportunity to object—to resist.

But she didn't.

He leaned forward. 'Carrie McKenzie, I'm going to kiss you now.' His voice was low, trying to entice her to edge forward to hear it.

But she didn't do that.

She did something totally unexpected. She lifted her hands and wrapped them around his neck. 'It's about time,' she whispered as she rose up on her toes to meet his lips.

Honey. She tasted of honey. Was there honey in the chocolate cake she'd just baked? At least that was what it felt like. The kiss started out shy—tentative. He didn't want her to feel forced. He didn't want her to feel as if she couldn't say no. He just prayed she wouldn't.

Her fingers wound up across his shorn hairline as the kiss deepened. As her tongue teased with his. Then she let out a little sigh that almost undid him completely.

He should pull back. He should let her out of his arms to give her time to think about this. There was still so much about Carrie McKenzie he didn't know.

But right now he didn't want to. Letting her go was the last thing he wanted to do right now. Not when she seemed to be matching him move for move.

And in an instant everything was black.

They jumped apart, then instantly moved back together again, bashing noses.

'Oops.' Carrie started to giggle as she rubbed her nose. 'I guess that will be the power cut, then.'

'I guess it is. Do you have any candles?'

'Yeah, I have some upstairs in my apartment. Not the emergency kind. More the bathroom kind.'

'What's a bathroom kind of candle?'

'The scented kind. The kind you light around your bath.'

He shook his head. 'I guess I'll take your word for it. We'll need something.'

'I'll go up and get them.'

He slipped his hand into hers. 'Let me come with you.'

'What about the baby?' She glanced over in the direction of the silent crib.

'Leave the door open. We'll only be a few minutes. He's sleeping. Nothing's going to happen.'

He liked holding her hand. It felt right inside his. It fitted.

They stumbled towards the door, leaving it wide open, and stepped out into the hallway. There was no light in the hall at all. No street lights shining in. No gentle glow underneath the opposite door. It was weird. He couldn't remember the last time there had been a power cut—probably why he didn't have any candles. He reached out for the banister and started up the stairs, giving her a gentle tug behind him.

They reached her door and she glanced in the direction of Mrs Van Dyke's apartment. 'Do you think we should check on her?'

'Maybe. Do you have any extra candles she could have?'

She let out a little laugh. 'Oh, I have a whole year's supply in here.' She pushed open the door to her apartment and walked over to the bathroom, bending down and pulling things from one of the cupboards.

Dan looked around as best he could. It took a few seconds for his eyes to adjust to the dark. The only available light was the moonlight outside, streaming in through one of the windows.

Neat. Tidy. Everything in its place.

There was nothing strange about that. Lots of women he knew were tidy. But there was something else. Something he couldn't quite put his finger on.

He moved across the room, putting his hand on the back of the leather sofa.

This wasn't Carrie's place, so she wouldn't have chosen any of the furnishings. But she'd been here for a few months now.

The darkness wasn't helping. Nor was the sight of Carrie's behind in her jeans as she bent over the cupboards and pulled out an array of candles.

She walked back over, fumbled through a drawer for a box of matches and lit the candle she was holding in a glass jar. The warm light spread up around her face, illuminating her like some TV movie star.

Candlelight suited her. Her pale skin glowed, her brown curly hair shiny and her eyes bright. She smiled as she held it out towards him and the aroma from the melting wax started to emerge.

He wrinkled his nose. 'What is that? Washing powder?'

She waved her hand in the air to waft the smell a little further. 'Close. Cotton fresh. I've also got lavender, orange, cinnamon, raspberry, spring dew and rain shower.'

'Sheesh. Who names these candles?'

She lit another one and moved over next to him again. 'I think it would be a great job. Right up there with naming paint shades.'

'You'd have a field day doing that.'

'You can bet on it. Imagine the fun. Shades of yellow—sunshine rays or daffodil petals. Shades of purple—sugared violet, lavender dreams or amethyst infusion.' Even in this dim light he could see the twinkle in her eyes and the enthusiasm in her voice were completely natural.

'Wow. You weren't joking, were you?' He took a little step closer.

She shook her head slowly. 'I don't know how the careers advisor missed it from my career matches.'

He could see her automatic reaction. She was drawn towards him.

A thought jumped into his head, tearing him away from the impure thoughts starting to filter through his brain. He groaned. 'What about the power? How can we sterilise the bottles and make the milk for Abraham?'

She touched his arm and an electric current shot straight up towards his shoulder, sending his brain straight back to his original thoughts. There was hesitation. She'd noticed it, too. 'We should be fine,' she said quietly, lifting her eyes slowly to meet his. 'I had just boiled the kettle and resterilised the bottles. We can make up one when we go back downstairs.' She was staring at him. Even in the dark light he could see the way her pupils had widened, taking over most of her eyes. Natural in the dark, but it didn't feel like that kind of response. It felt like another entirely.

He set his candle down on a nearby side table, letting the glow shine upwards, emphasising the curve of her breasts and hips. He couldn't pretend any more. He couldn't hide his reactions. He didn't want to.

He put his hand on her hip, pulling her closer, leaving her with a candle jar clutched to her chest. 'So, not only am I marooned here—' he waved his other hand around '—in a snowstorm, with the power out, with a lady who found a baby on the doorstep and knows all the words to every musical known to man—' his hand came back to rest on her other hip, pulling her even closer with only the burning candle between them '—I find out she's also slightly crazy. With career ambitions even the career-matching machine couldn't have predicted.'

There was hesitancy there. A little apprehension—even though they had been lip-locked a few minutes ago. But Carrie was gradually relaxing. He could feel the tension leaving her arms and her body easing into his. She moved the flickering candle from between them, pressing her warm breasts against his chest. If she moved any more, things could start to get out of hand.

But she was smiling. A happy, relaxed smile. A warm smile. The kind he'd only glimpsed on a few rare occasions over the past two days. The kind that showed she'd let her guard down. The metal portcullis that was kept firmly in place was starting to ease up—ever so gently.

It revealed the real Carrie McKenzie. The kind of person she could be—if she was brave enough. The kind of person he'd like to know more about—be it vertical or horizontal.

Stop it! He tried to push those thoughts from his crowded head. Carrie just wasn't that kind of girl. And instead of lessening the attraction it only heightened it.

He reached up and pulled one of her long chestnut curls from behind her ear. 'I like your hair down. It's beautiful. Really flattering.' He hesitated a second as his finger brushed the side of her face. He didn't want to push this. He didn't want to scare her off.

Even though his male urges were giving him a whole other vibe his brain kept jumping in to keep him in check. 'Sexy,' he murmured, holding his breath to see the effect of his words.

He could almost predict she would tense and pull away. It was the biggest part of Carrie that he'd seen over the past couple of days.

But something had changed. The dim lights, the candles or just her new relaxed state meant that instead of pulling away she brushed closer against him and rested her hands on his shoulders. 'Sexy—I like that.' Her breath was dancing against his skin. He had to let her be the one to make the move. He had to be sure about this.

Those few seconds seemed like forever.

But she did move. Her body pressed against his a little more firmly and he felt her rise up on her tiptoes. Her lips brushed gently against his, then with a little more confidence her kisses became surer. His hands moved to her ribs; he could feel her deep breaths against the palms of his hands. He couldn't stop them. He wanted to do more.

She had one hand on his back, the other at

the side of his face as she deepened their kiss, teasing him with her tongue.

It was driving him crazy. *She* was driving him crazy.

He wanted to release the emotions and passions that were currently stifled in his chest doing their best impression of a smouldering volcano. But Carrie had to feel in control. He could sense how important that was.

He had to concentrate. He couldn't lose himself in this. It was far too tempting. Far too tempting by half.

All he had to do was edge his hands a little higher and then he would feel her warm skin, be able to cup the warm mounds of her breasts and...

He stepped back. Slowly, pulling his lips apart from hers. Careful to let her know he hadn't suddenly changed his mind about this.

His voice was hoarse. Too much pent-up expectation. 'I hate to remind you, Carrie McKenzie, but we have a sleeping baby downstairs. We've only been gone a few minutes but if you distract me for another second...' He let his voice drift off, leaving her in no doubt as to his meaning.

He wasn't pulling away from her because he didn't want to kiss her.

He was pulling away because right now he *should*.

She bit her lip.

A tiny movement. And one that could be the complete undoing of him. He wanted to slam her apartment door shut and drag her through to the bedroom. And forget about everything else and everyone.

But on the floor underneath them lay a little boy. He'd already been abandoned by one adult. He certainly didn't need to be abandoned by two others.

Daniel's sense of duty ground down on his chest.

He tugged at his jeans, trying to adjust them. Some human reactions were as natural as breathing.

Others he would have to control.

She nodded. 'Let me grab a few things that I might need.' She picked up one of the candles and walked over to her bedroom, opening a cupboard and pulling a few items of clothing out.

In the flickering candlelight he could make out the outline of her bed and possessions scattered around the room. A smile danced across his lips. Carrie McKenzie's bedroom. Would he ever get an invite into there?

It wasn't entirely what he'd expected. No flowers. No pink.

A bright green duvet, a mountain of pillows and a matching fleece comforter across the bottom of the bed. An electronic tablet and a few books were scattered on the bedside table, along with a few other obligatory candles. He wondered what scent they were. What scent she liked to fall asleep to.

A silver box lay on top of the bedclothes.

Her eyes flickered over to it and there was something—was it panic?—before she moved quickly, picked up the box and tucked it under the bed. She tucked the assorted clothes under her arm and appeared under his nose. 'Ready.'

It was just a little too bright. A little too forced. As if she was trying to distract him.

He'd just been kissing this woman but there were still parts of her she wanted to keep hidden. A tiny flare of anger lit in his stomach, only for him to extinguish it almost as quickly. He should know better than most. Everyone had secrets they wanted to hide. Parts of their life they wanted to remain hidden. Why should Carrie be any different?

'Let's go. We need to check on Abraham, and Mrs Van Dyke.'

He turned to follow her out of the door. And then it hit him.

That was what was wrong with this place.

There was nothing really of *Carrie*.

Oh, she might have her candles and a few books.

But there were no photos. Not a single one.

It sent a strange sensation down his spine. Every woman he'd ever known had pictures of their friends and family dotted around. Even he had some family pictures in various places around his apartment.

Carrie didn't have one. Not a single one.

What did that mean? She'd been here two months, surely enough time to get some family snaps out. Wasn't there anyone to miss back home?

'Dan, what's wrong? Let's go.' Carrie stuck her head back around the door, her impatience clear. Or was it her hurry to get him out of her apartment?

With one last look around he followed her out and pulled the door shut behind him.

There was more to Carrie McKenzie than met the eye.

And he was determined to get to the bottom of it.

CHAPTER SEVEN

WHEN CARRIE OPENED her eyes that morning it was to a totally different sight.

Blue walls and white bed linen.

The disorientation was over in an instant. She drew in a deep breath. It was strange waking up in someone else's bed.

She'd felt like that the first few nights in the apartment upstairs. Then, after a week, she hadn't even noticed. It just proved to her how much *home* in London hadn't really felt like *home* any more.

Dan's place was much more lived-in than hers. But then, he'd spent most of his life here. In amongst the state-of-the-art television and digital sound system, there were tiny ornaments, old picture frames and the odd piece of antique furniture. The little dark wood side table next to the door was her favourite. He hadn't really said much about how he'd ended up living with his grandmother and she didn't want to pry.

Just as she didn't want him to pry too much, either.

An unconscious smile crept across her face. He'd kissed her.

And she'd kissed him back.

Her first kiss since…

And it felt nice. It felt good.

Actually it felt a lot more than all that. Nice and good made it sound like a safe kiss. A kiss that was taking her on the road to recovery.

But Dan's kiss had ignited a whole lot more than that in her. She almost couldn't sleep last night when they'd parted. It was amazing how long you could lie staring up at the ceiling while your brain was on a spin cycle.

She looked around the room. A pair of his boots were on the floor, along with a pair of jeans slung across a chair. She could almost still see the shape of his body in those jeans. And it sent another lot of little pulses skittering across her skin.

Dan had decided to do the night shift last night. She was almost sure another two slices of her chocolate cake had been the appropriate bribe for him to spend the night on his lumpy sofa.

Abraham. He appeared in her thoughts like a flash and she sat upright in bed.

She hadn't heard him. She hadn't heard him at all.

A chill spread across her body instantly, reaching straight down into the pit of her stomach. Sending its icy tendrils around her heart.

No. Surely not.

She was up and out of the bedroom before her feet even felt as if they'd touched the wooden floor. Her steps across the floor the quickest she'd ever moved. Her breath caught in her throat and she leaned over the crib.

Empty. It was empty.

She spun around. 'Dan—' And stopped dead.

Dan was upright on the sofa, fast asleep with Abraham tucked against his shoulder. She'd obviously missed quite a bit last night. Why hadn't he woken her up? More importantly, why hadn't she heard?

In her haste across the room she hadn't even looked over at his slumped frame. She'd been so focused on Abraham. So focused on the baby.

Dan's eyes flickered open and he lifted his hand covered in the cast to rub his sleep-ridden eyes. 'Wake my baby and I'll kill you,' he growled, echoing her words from the day before.

'I'm sorry,' she gasped. 'I just woke up and

realised I hadn't heard him all night. I thought something was wrong. Then he wasn't in the crib and I—' She stopped to draw breath, conscious of the look on Dan's face. 'What? What is it?'

The coldness of the wooden floor was starting to seep through her toes and up her legs, making goosebumps erupt on her skin—her woefully exposed skin.

'Oh!' She lifted her arms across her breasts. Some body reactions weren't for public view.

Dan had been right about her other nightwear. Her tiny satin nightie covered her bum and not much more. Last night she'd been wearing her dressing gown—her eternal protection—and hadn't removed it until she'd climbed into bed. The power had come back on and the temperature in the apartment was warmer than usual, both having agreed that due to the lack of appropriate clothing for Abraham they needed to raise the temperature slightly. So she couldn't have bundled up in her usual fleece pyjamas—not without melting completely—and Dan would never see her in her nightie anyway, would he? Until now.

The cold floor had the ultimate effect on her body. Her nipples were firmly pressed into the sides of her arms across her chest. They had obviously been the feature that had caught his attention.

'Give me a second,' she blurted as she made a run for the bedroom and the sanctity of her dressing gown. Too late she realised how much her slight nightie must have flapped around her behind, leaving little to the imagination.

She emerged a few minutes later, trying not to look completely flustered.

'I'll make breakfast this morning,' she said brightly. 'It was American yesterday—you made pancakes. So I think it will be tea, toast and marmalade this morning.'

Dan couldn't wipe the smile off his face, even though she was trying desperately to change the earlier subject. He shook his head. 'I sense distraction techniques, Carrie McKenzie. But since I'm a gentleman with an empty stomach I'll let it go. As for toast and marmalade? No, you don't. You sabotaged the pancakes with your butter and jam. And don't even think about making me tea after the night I've had. I need coffee. With at least three shots.'

Guilt surged through her and she sat down next to him. She was safe now; she was completely covered. 'Was Abraham really bad last night? I'm so sorry. I never heard a thing.'

'I noticed.' He shook his head and gave her a weary smile. 'If I'd needed you, Carrie, I would have woken you up. But it was fine.' He paused. 'Well, actually, it wasn't fine, but I closed the door so you wouldn't hear. I figured this was hard enough for you and a night with no sleep wouldn't help.'

She was stunned.

It was no secret she hadn't managed to hide things from Dan. He'd already asked her on more than one occasion what was wrong and she hadn't responded. Because she didn't feel ready to.

It had only been a few days. And she didn't know him that well—not really. But Dan had taken actions last night to make sure she had some respite. He was reading her better than she could have ever thought. Was it the cop instincts? Did he just know when to push and when to back off?

Did they even teach things like that in cop school? Or was he just good at reading her? At sensing when things were tough and she needed to step back. She wasn't ready to share. Or was she?

Her friends back home all knew about the stillbirth. And they either tiptoed around her or tried to make her talk. Neither way worked for her.

She needed to talk when *she* was ready. Not when they were ready.

Maybe it would be easier to share with someone from outside her circle of friends. Someone who could be impartial and not try to hit her with a whole host of advice about what to do and how she should feel.

Dan was the first guy to cause her stomach to flutter in a whole year. She'd thought that part of her had died. And nothing would cause it to wake up again. But the close proximity was definitely a factor. How much of a risk would it be to tell him, to trust him?

Looking at the snow outside, they could be here for at least another whole day. The flickering TV in the corner of the room still had the yellow strip running across the news report, telling about more snowfall and more people cut off from their family and friends. 'I see there's going to be more snow.' She nodded at the TV.

He sighed. 'Yeah.' He shrugged his shoulders as his eyes met hers. 'Seems like we're not going anywhere fast.'

'At least the electric shower will be working. And the kettle and hob. I'll be able to sterilise things and make some more bottles for Abraham.' The practical things. The things that always came into her brain first.

But there was something else there. Something else drumming away inside her head.

They were stuck here. For at least another day. Another day with delectable Dan.

Another day with a baby. Could she cope? Could she do this again?

It was as if something happened inside. A little flare sparked inside her brain. This was it. This was her chance.

If only she had the courage.

She held out her hands towards Abraham. Would Dan notice they were trembling? 'May I?'

He nodded and handed over the half-sleeping babe to her. Abraham didn't seem to mind who was holding him. He snuggled instantly into her shoulder, obviously preferring the upright position.

There was a loud splurging noise, closely followed by a smell creeping around the apartment. Carrie wrinkled her nose. 'Oh, Abraham. How could you?'

Her hand felt along his back and came into contact with a little splurge at the side of the nappy and halfway up his back. She let out a sigh and set him down in the crib.

'I guess it's going to be a bath for you, little sir.'

'How are we going to manage that? We don't have a baby bath.'

Carrie walked over to the deep kitchen sink.

'We'll improvise. This is the best we've got. Don't you remember ever getting bathed in the kitchen sink as a child?'

He shook his head. 'Can't say that I do. Is it an English tradition?'

Carrie had started to scrub the sink within an inch of her life. 'I guess it must be, then. My gran's got some pictures of me sitting bare naked in her kitchen sink. I thought everyone did that.'

She filled the sink with some tepid water and baby bubble bath before testing the temperature. She stripped Abraham's clothes and put them in a bucket of cold water to soak. Dan wrinkled his nose. 'I'm going to wash these? Really? Wouldn't it be better just putting them in the garbage?'

Carrie shook her head. 'We don't have that luxury, Dan. We only have a few things that fit him. They'll just need to be soaked and then boil washed.'

Dan lifted the bucket and headed down to the laundry. 'Be back in five,' he said.

Carrie lifted Abraham from the towel he was squirming on. 'Let's see if we can get this all off you,' she said as she gently lowered him into the warm water.

The expression on his face was priceless. First he squirmed. Then he let out a little yelp of dismay. It only lasted for a few seconds before the shock of being cold disappeared and his little body picked up the surrounding warm water. He gave a little shudder. Then started to kick his legs.

She smiled. His first baby bath.

Her first baby bath. And it was just the two of them.

There was something about it that was so nice. She knew this should be a moment that he shared with his mother. But it was almost as if this were meant to be. She watched as his little legs stretched out and kicked in the water in the sink. She lapped the water over his stomach and chest. He let out a range of little noises. If she didn't know better she could imagine he was almost smiling.

Some babies screamed when they hit the bathwater, hating being stripped of their warm cocoonlike clothes. But not Abraham. He seemed to relish it, enjoying kicking his legs in the water.

She lifted some cotton wool balls, being careful to make sure he was entirely clean. Turning his position slightly, so she could make sure there was nothing left on his back.

That was when it happened.

That was when he gave a little judder.

She knew instinctively something was wrong.

She turned him over, her hands struggling to hold his slippery body as she panicked. He was pale. Deathly pale. Almost as if he was holding his breath.

No. No!

She let out a scream. She couldn't help it. The whole world had just started to close in all around her. She grabbed him beneath the arms and thrust the dripping baby into Dan's arms as he strode back through the door.

'Carrie, what's wrong?'

She couldn't stop. She couldn't breathe. Her feet carried her outside the apartment door and out onto the steps. The cold snow-covered steps where she'd found him. As soon as she reached the cold air it was as if her legs gave way and she collapsed down onto the steps, struggling to catch her breath.

There were tiny little black spots around her vision. She put her head between her legs and told herself to breathe slowly. But nothing could stop the clamouring in her chest.

That sight. That pale little body. That still little chest. It had been too much for her. That momentary second of panic had made her head spin. No one should have to go through that twice in their life.

No one was meant to experience that again.

Breathe. In through her nose, out through

her mouth. And again. Breathe. In through her nose and out through her mouth.

She tried to get control. Her senses were picking up something else. A noise. A background noise. A baby crying.

Then she started to sob. Uncontrollably sob. Abraham was fine. She knew that. She'd panicked. If she'd stopped to think—even for a moment—she would have realised he'd only been holding his breath for a second. But she couldn't. She didn't possess those rational kinds of thoughts any more. And she doubted she ever would.

Then she felt it, a hand creeping around her shoulders and a body sitting on the step next to her. The heat of another body touching hers. The comfort of an arm around her shoulders and the feeling of somewhere she could lay her head.

But he didn't speak. Dan just held her. She didn't know how long passed. She didn't know how long she sobbed. All she knew was his arms were around her and he was holding her— as if he would never let go.

His hand was stroking her hair. It was bitter cold out here, but neither of them seemed to notice. 'Tell me, Carrie,' he whispered. 'Tell me how to help you.'

'You can't, Dan.' It was a relief to say the

words out loud. 'I panicked. I thought Abraham had stopped breathing.'

'He's fine, Carrie. Abraham is absolutely fine.' His voice washed over her, like a calm, soothing tonic. He lifted her chin towards his face. 'But you're not.' His finger traced the track of tears down her cheek. 'You're not fine, Carrie. Tell me why not.'

It was time. It was time to tell the truth. 'Why do you struggle with babies?'

The million-dollar question.

'Because I had one.'

She heard his intake of breath, but to his credit he never reacted the way she expected. There was a few moments' silence while he obviously contemplated her news. 'When did you have one?' His voice was low, comforting. The question wasn't intrusive. He made it feel like an everyday conversation.

'Last year.'

'Oh.'

'Yes, oh.' A shiver danced along her spine. Was it a reaction to the cold? Or was it a reaction to saying those words out loud?

Dan stood up and pulled her along with him. 'Let's do this inside. Let's do this inside with Abraham.'

Even now he didn't want to leave the baby on

his own. Dan was being a good parent. It made this seem so much easier.

Abraham was wrapped in a towel, his bare toes kicking at the air above. As Dan closed the door behind them, shutting out the cold winter air, she knew what she had to do. She knew what would help her through this.

She picked up the kicking bundle and held him close to her chest, taking some deep breaths in and out.

She couldn't think of a single reason why this made her feel better. The thought of holding another baby in her arms had terrified her for so long. But the past few days had been cathartic.

Never, in a million years, would she have thought that holding another baby in her arms while she talked about the one she had lost would feel okay. Would actually feel quite right. If she'd ever planned to share, it would never have been like this.

'It wasn't too long ago.' Her words were firmer than she expected. She'd always thought that she'd never be able to get them out.

Maybe it was because she was with Dan. Maybe it was because he was literally a captive audience with no place to go. Maybe it was because she knew he couldn't run out on her if he didn't like what she heard. Maybe it was because she was beginning to feel as if she could tell this guy anything.

'Fifteenth of May last year, I had a little girl. Ruby. She was stillborn.'

There was silence.

It seemed important. Even though she hated the word *stillborn* it seemed important to her to tell him what had happened to her baby. She didn't want him to think she'd given her baby up for adoption, or done the same as Abraham's mother and abandoned her.

What was he thinking? And then a warm hand crept up and covered hers, squeezing gently. 'I'm sorry you lost your daughter, Carrie. That must have been a terrible time for you.'

The quiet acknowledgement made tears spring to her eyes. 'Thank you, Dan,' she whispered.

For Ruby. He was expressing his sorrow for the loss of her daughter. For Ruby. Some people didn't like to acknowledge a baby who had been lost. Some people didn't even want to say their names. It was easier to pretend they'd never existed. After all, babies who had never drawn breath in this world, they practically hadn't been here.

Except Ruby had been here.

She'd kicked under her mother's expanding stomach for seven months. She'd twisted and turned in the middle of the night, constantly having dancing competitions that kept her mother awake into the small hours. Sometimes a little foot or hand had been clearly visible as Carrie had lain watching her belly.

Ruby McKenzie had definitely existed. And it was so nice to finally talk about her. Talk about her in a normal way instead of in hushed, quiet tones.

'Is that what's in the silver box upstairs?'

Now he had surprised her. 'How do you know about the box?'

'I saw it sitting on your bed when we were in your apartment. I saw the way you looked at it.' He gave her a little smile. 'It's pretty. And it seemed important.' His finger traced along the knuckles of her hand, small circular motions. 'Your place. You didn't have pictures up. For a woman, that struck me as strange. I figured you had a good reason and didn't want to ask.'

A tear slid down her cheek. 'I'm trying to get away from memories. That's why I'm in New York. It seemed like a good time to get away. Everything and everyone back home just reminded me of last year. It made sense. Coming here, getting away from it all.'

Dan traced his finger from her hand to her breastbone. His voice was intense. 'You can't get away from what's in here, Carrie. It stays with you all the time—no matter where you go.'

Wow. Her breath caught in her throat.

It was the way he said the words. The understanding. How could Dan be so in tune with things? There was an intensity she hadn't seen before. A darkening of his brown eyes from caramel tones to deep chocolate colours.

He knew. He understood her straight away, and she didn't know why.

'I know that. But sometimes what's in here feels easier if you've got room to deal with it yourself.' Easier than everyone clamouring around you, suffocating you with *their* grief.

'And has it been? Has it been easier, Carrie?'

'I thought it was. I thought I was coming to terms with things.' Her eyes went down to Abraham. 'Until now. Until him.' She could hear the waver in her voice, feel the tremble in her throat. She desperately wanted to keep it together. She wanted to put her thoughts, feelings and frustrations into words—in a way she'd never managed before.

But Dan's reaction was flooring her. She couldn't have asked for more.

Dan shook his head. 'No wonder you didn't want to help out. No wonder you tried to make excuses.' His eyes were still heavy with weariness and she could see the lines on his face.

He was fighting fatigue with every bone in his body.

He turned around on the sofa so he was facing her entirely. 'I'm sorry, Carrie. I had no idea how hard this was for you. But I really needed your help. I couldn't do this on my own. I don't know the first thing about babies.'

The gentle tears were still flowing. 'And neither do I, Dan. I never got the chance to find out. And I'm so worried I'll do something wrong. What if I caused Ruby to be stillborn? What if it was something I did? Something I ate? I'm not sure I should be around babies. I'm terrified that I'll do something wrong. What if he's sick and I don't know it? What if the jaundice gets worse instead of better?' She shook her head. 'I've already held one dead baby in my arms. I couldn't live with myself if anything happened to Abraham.'

Panic was welling up inside her and threatening to take over.

Some things were still too much for her. Still too raw.

Dan put his hands on her shoulders. 'Don't, Carrie. Don't do this to yourself. We've spoken to Shana. You heard what she said. As soon as possible, she'll arrange to examine Abraham and make sure everything is fine. Nothing happened today when you bathed him. Abraham must have just held his breath. As soon as you handed him to me, it was almost as if he let out a little squawk. It was nothing you did, Carrie. Nothing at all. As for doing something wrong— I'm more likely to do that than you. You're a natural. Everything you do is right. No matter how hard you're finding this, you still make a much better parent than I do. I couldn't even get a diaper on straight!' He pressed his fingers into the tops of her arms. 'I don't know what happened to Ruby, but I don't believe for a second it was your fault. Did they ever tell you? What did the medical examiner say?'

Carrie took a deep breath. 'Nothing. They found nothing. Although she was early Ruby was the right size and weight. There was nothing wrong with my placenta. There was nothing wrong with the umbilical cord. I hadn't been in an accident. I didn't have any infections. My blood pressure was fine. They couldn't give me a single reason why Ruby stopped moving that day. She was perfect. She was perfect in every way.'

Her voice was cracking now. Her head was filling with pictures of that room. The expression on the radiographer's face as she swept Carrie's abdomen, trying to find a heartbeat with no success. The quiet way she had spoken, mentioning she needed to look for a colleague before disappearing out of the door.

And Carrie, sitting in the semi-dark room, knowing, just *knowing,* that life was about to change in an unimaginable way. Placing her hands on her stomach, ignoring the gel, and just talking to her baby. Telling her that Mummy loved her. Forever and ever.

Ruby's name had been picked weeks before. The hand-painted letters already adorned the door of the room in their flat that had been dedicated as the nursery. The nursery that Ruby would never see—never live in.

She could see the empathy on Dan's face. He understood. He understood the pure frustration of having no reason, no answer to the worst thing that could happen to her.

He lifted his heavy eyelids with caution. 'What about Ruby's dad?'

'What about Ruby's dad?' She shook her head. A small bit of guilt still weighed on her soul. 'Mark was a good guy. But neither of us could cope with what happened. Things just fell apart. He got another job and moved away. He's met someone now. And I'm happy for him. We just couldn't stay together—it was far too hard. Like having a permanent reminder etched on your brain.'

'Seems to me that Ruby will be permanently

etched on your brain anyhow. Whether you're with Mark or not.'

She stared at him. That was blunt and to the point. And for the first time Dan had a deep crease across his forehead. A crease she wanted to reach up and smooth away with her fingers.

She was feeling it. This connection to Dan. Just as he was feeling it, too.

Mark was a chapter of her life that was over. And although she thought about Ruby frequently, she barely ever thought about Mark.

Dan's last remark seemed almost protective, and a tiny bit territorial. And the strangest thing was she didn't mind. Why had she been so scared to talk about this?

It wasn't comfortable. It wasn't comfortable at all. But Dan seemed to understand more than she would have expected him to.

And Dan was everything Mark wasn't. Mark couldn't bear to be around her once she'd lost Ruby. It was too hard. Too hard for them both. But Dan was nothing like that. She couldn't imagine Mark in this situation. Looking after an abandoned baby. Mark would have wanted nothing to do with that at all. But Dan had taken it all in his stride. A totally different kind of man.

And timing was everything. If New York hadn't been hit by this freak snowstorm she and Dan might never have talked. Might never have got to know each other and started to show these little glimmers of trust.

She sagged back on the sofa as Abraham let out a little sigh, his warm breath against her neck. 'I don't ever want to forget my daughter, Daniel. I couldn't, and I wouldn't ever want to. I have things in the box, her first scan, her scan at twenty weeks. A few little things that I'd bought for her that she never got to wear.' She stared off into the distance. 'I had to buy something new. Something for very premature babies to put on her. And some photos. I have some photos. But—'

She broke off, unable to finish. The photographs were just too painful.

His hand was wrapped back around hers again. 'So, how do you feel about helping me with Abraham? I know it's hard for you, Carrie. But I really need your help.' His words were said with caution, as if he didn't want to cause her any more pain.

She took a few moments before she answered, trying to sort it all out in her brain. 'It's strange. It's not quite what I'd expected. I've avoided babies for months. Any of my friends who were pregnant and delivered, I just made excuses not to see them and sent a present. I think they all understood. Most of them felt awkward around me anyway. I thought Abraham would be my worst nightmare.'

'And?'

'And—' she looked down at the little face, snuggled against her shoulder '—I won't pretend it's not hard. I won't pretend that I don't sometimes just need a minute. Just need a little space. But it's not as bad as I expected.'

The heat from Abraham's little body was penetrating through her dressing gown, like an additional hot-water bottle. But it felt good. It felt natural. It didn't make her want to run screaming from the room. Not in the way she would have expected.

'Then can you do this, Carrie? Can you keep helping me for the next day or so?' He pointed to the TV. 'It doesn't look like New York is opening back up for business any time soon.' He touched her arm, and she could sense the frustration he was trying to hide from her. 'I'll understand, Carrie. I'll understand if you say no and want to go back up to your apartment and stay there.'

She thought about it. There was no hiding the fact that for a few moments she actually considered it. But just at that point Abraham moved and snuggled even closer to her neck.

What was up there for her? An empty apartment with no one to talk to. There was only so much news she could watch on TV saying the same things over and over again.

There were only so many times she could rearrange her wardrobe and shoes. There were only so many times she could reread her favourite books.

She sucked in a deep breath. He was watching her. *He* was holding *his* breath, waiting for her response. 'You understand now, but you didn't understand a couple of nights ago.' She could remember the stunned expression on his face when she'd bolted for the door.

He nodded in defeat. 'You're right. I thought you were distinctly weird. But I was crazy and desperate enough not to care.' He pointed to his chest. 'But I know, Carrie, I know in here if someone is a good person. And don't think it's anything about being a cop. I've been like this since I was a kid. I always knew who had a good heart—no matter what their appearance or surroundings. And I always knew who to steer clear of, no matter what they told me.'

There were shadows in his eyes. He was revealing a tiny part of himself here. Maybe without even knowing it. And that was the second time this had happened. First with the comment about things always staying inside you, and now about knowing people—who to stay away from. How had he learned that lesson? It was painful to even think about it.

She reached up and touched the side of his face with her free hand. Bristles. Dan hadn't managed to shave yet and they felt good beneath her smooth skin. She even liked the sound.

'And do you want to steer clear of me, Dan?' He was staring at her with those dark brown eyes. Pulling her in. Thank goodness she was sitting or her legs would currently be like jelly.

There was comfort here. Because she knew what he was about to say. Didn't doubt it for a second. This connection was the truest thing she'd felt in a long time.

He gave her that sexy smile. The one that made her stomach flip over. 'Not for a second,' he whispered, and leaned forward and brushed his lips against hers.

It was beautiful. The gentlest of kisses.

Just as well. She still had Abraham in her arms. Under any other circumstances she might feel the urge to throw her dressing gown to the wind and jump up onto his lap.

He was concentrating solely on her mouth. His hand still only brushing the side of her face as their kiss deepened and his tongue edged its way into her mouth.

She could feel the heat rush through her,

warming her chilled legs and feet and spreading to a whole host of other places.

She could concentrate solely on this. She could concentrate solely on Dan. Once he started kissing her nothing else mattered. Her brain didn't have room for a single thought.

But as if sensing where this could go, Dan pulled back.

And for a second she felt lost. Until she opened her eyes again and realised he was smiling at her.

'What do you think, Carrie McKenzie? Will you be my partner in crime? Can Abraham and I count on you?'

She narrowed her eyes at him. Boy, he was good. With his fancy words and his kisses. His help-the-baby plea. This man could charm the birds out of the trees.

Just as well she was the only bird around.

She lifted her eyebrows. 'Are you doing this for the chocolate cake?'

He smiled. 'I'm definitely doing it for the chocolate cake.'

'Well, that makes us even, 'cause I'm doing this for the carrot cake—and the pancakes.' She liked this. She liked that they could fall back into flirting so easily, even after her monumental revelation.

'Just what I like—a woman with her priorities in order.' He pushed himself up from the sofa and held out his hands for Abraham.

'Don't you want me to take a turn for a while?'

'Oh, no.' He shook his head firmly as he gathered Abraham into his arms and took a long look at her bare legs and painted toenails. 'What I want is for you to put some clothes on. You're *way* too distracting without them.'

She stood up, deliberately letting her dressing gown open, just to annoy him. 'Well, we wouldn't want any distractions, would we?' she teased as she headed to the door.

There was some colour in his cheeks. A guy like Dan couldn't be embarrassed. Not when he looked like that. He must have women throwing themselves at him all the time—particularly when he was in uniform.

She saw him shifting uncomfortably, adjusting himself. No! She'd caused an age-old reaction with a few cheeky words and a flash of skin. Her cheeks started to blush, too.

And then she started to smile.

It was starting to feel as if she had some control back. As if everything in life wouldn't just slip through her fingers like grains of sand on the beach.

She turned the handle on the door.

'Carrie?'

She spun around.

Dan was standing with Abraham in his arms. Looking every inch the gorgeous family man. Looking every inch like the man she pictured in her dreams about the life she wanted to have.

'Hurry back.'

She tried to think of something witty or clever to say. But she had nothing.

'Absolutely,' she muttered as she sped up the stairs as fast as her legs would carry her.

Her brain had just flipped into a spin cycle again.

It was certifiable. Daniel Cooper was driving her crazy.

CHAPTER EIGHT

By now Dan should have been a crumpled heap on the floor. He'd spent most of last night walking the floor with a sometimes whimpering, sometimes screaming baby. At one point he'd put Abraham back in the crib and gone to stand in the kitchen for a few minutes to catch his breath.

But from the moment Carrie had appeared, all bright-eyed and bushy-tailed after a good night's sleep, he'd felt instantly invigorated.

There was something about her brown curls, blue eyes and flash of skin that was slowly but surely driving him crazy.

And now he knew.

Now he understood.

Well, not entirely. God willing he'd never really understand what it felt like to lose a child. But at least now he had an explanation for the shadows beneath her eyes. The moments of panic that he'd seen and recognised. Her abruptness. Her lack of confidence in herself.

What he couldn't understand was why Carrie couldn't see what he could see. A remarkably caring and competent woman who seemed to have a real empathy with this little baby.

For some reason Carrie's news reassured him a little. He'd known there was something wrong but hadn't quite been able to put his finger on it. His instincts told him she was a good person and not a crazed baby-snatcher or madly unstable.

Carrie McKenzie was probably the bravest woman he'd ever met. And that included his grandmother.

She'd put the needs of this little baby—a child she didn't know—before her own needs, even though it was apparent at times her heart was clearly breaking. How many other people did he know who could have done this?

A smile danced across his lips as he remembered her reaction to Shana's 'suck it up' comment. No wonder she'd been so horrified.

This was truly her worst nightmare and she'd just lived through thirty-odd hours of it, with only a few minor hiccups along the way.

He'd been right to let her sleep. It seemed to have given her new strength and the confidence to share. And he was glad she'd shared.

He'd just resisted the temptation to gather her into his arms and try to take her pain away. Because something told him this was all new for her. Sharing about this was all new for her, and he had to let her go at her own pace.

And while it seemed the most unlikely solution, holding Abraham had seemed to give her comfort at that moment. Which was why he'd resorted to the smallest movement—the hand squeeze—to show his support.

What did this mean now for them?

Now that she'd shared he'd given her the opportunity to walk away. To stop making things so hard on herself. But she was determined to stay and help. And his sense of relief was overwhelming. If left to himself, he was sure he could muddle through. But having someone else there—even a little reluctantly—was more help than she could imagine.

As for the kiss?

How much was Carrie ready to move on?

Because being in a confined space with her was going to drive him crazy—in a good way. Now that he'd tasted her sweet lips and felt the warmth of her body next to his it just made him crave her all the more.

Carrie wasn't like any other woman that he'd met.

Girls in New York weren't shy. *Reserved* was an extinct term around here.

He was used to women throwing themselves at him, in pursuit of either a relationship or something far hotter.

It was just the way of the world these days.

But truth be told, it wasn't really Dan's world. It wasn't really the family values his grandmother had brought him up with. They, in themselves, were almost laughable. His mother certainly hadn't had any family values—no matter what her family had taught her. And that had reflected badly on Dan.

His grandmother had patched him up, fought fiercely for him and his mother's name was never mentioned in the house again.

And that was fine with him. For years she haunted his dreams most nights anyway.

But Carrie McKenzie, with her too-blue eyes and quiet nature, was slowly but surely getting under his skin in a way no other woman had.

It was clear there were some aspects of life they disagreed on. But did that mean it would be pointless to pursue anything else? Dan wasn't sure. He still had his own demons to deal with. And the situation with Abraham was only heightening a whole host of emotions he'd buried for so long.

His stomach grumbled loudly just as Carrie

burst back through the door, wearing a pink shirt and jeans, her hair tied up in a loose knot. She laughed at the sound of his stomach. 'You called?'

He nodded at her hands that were clutched to her chest holding a jar of lemon marmalade. 'It's getting to the stage I won't even fight you about the toast and marmalade. You've starved me so long I'm ready to concede.' He walked over to the crib and laid Abraham back down.

She strode over to the toaster and slid the last of the bread into place. 'I'll concede on one thing. I'll make you coffee instead of tea—but only since you had such a bad night. I might make some scones this afternoon and make you drink tea, then.'

He felt his ears literally prick up. The cupboards' supplies were getting low—even though it had only been a few days. The cakes yesterday had been a real boost. Scones today? Even better.

'I've never really had the scone things. What do you have them with?'

She shrugged. 'It should be jam and cream, but jam and butter will do. Do you want fruit scones or plain?'

He rolled his eyes upwards. 'I take it bacon's not an option?' He smiled at the horrified expression on her face. 'You've got a secret stash of dried fruit up there, too?'

She put her hand on her hip and gave him a sassy look. 'I've got a whole host of things you know nothing about up there.'

He let out a stream of air through his lips. 'Woman, you're going to drive me crazy.'

The toast popped behind her and she started spreading butter and marmalade, pulled out two plates and mugs and finished making breakfast in record time.

It was almost as if Abraham had an inbuilt antenna. As soon as Carrie's backside hovered above the chair he started to grizzle in his crib. She glanced at the clock. 'When did he have his last feed?'

Dan looked at his watch. 'I think it was around four. This little guy is like clockwork. He couldn't possibly let it go any more than four hours.'

'It must be my turn to feed him. Let me make up a bottle.' She picked out the bottle and teat from the sterilising solution and measured out the formula. 'I wish we could get some more of the ready-made formula. It's so much easier.' She peered into the contents of the formula tub. 'How many bottles does this make? I know it's only a small can but it seems to be going down mighty quickly.' She turned back to face him.

Dan wasn't listening. He was staring at the toast and lemon marmalade as if it had sprouted legs and run across the floor.

'Dan? Dan? What's wrong.'

He took another bite of the toast. 'This is much nicer than I remember. Or maybe it's just that I'm so hungry that I would eat anything.' He stared at the toast. 'I always thought marmalade was—you know—yeuch.' He let a shiver go down his spine. 'I don't remember it tasting like this.'

She gave him a smile. 'It's one of my secrets. You probably had orange marmalade as a child. I don't like it, either. This is much nicer, made with lemons. I brought it with me from London.'

He narrowed his eyes. 'Where do you keep the jar?'

She tapped the side of her nose. 'Aha, that's a secret. You'll never make me tell.'

'Never?' He stood up, his chair skidding across the floor and his hands on her hips in an instant. She could hardly even remember him crossing the space.

Oh, no. Those come-to-bed eyes again. The kind that gave her ideas she really shouldn't be having at this time of day.

He didn't wait. He didn't ask. He just claimed her lips as his own. His hand coming up and cupping her cheek. There was an element of ownership in his actions.

But the strange thing was, instead of being annoying, it sent little sparks of heat all the way down to the tips of her toes.

The past year had been lonely. The past year had been more than lonely. The past year had been dark and bleak and, at times, scary.

Sometimes she felt as if the black cloud around her would never lift, no matter how hard she tried.

For the first time she was feeling something other than despair. Other than hopelessness.

Maybe her senses were overreacting. Maybe it had just been too long since she'd been in a position like this, where her hormones couldn't keep themselves in check.

All she knew was she wanted Daniel Cooper's lips on hers. She wanted Daniel Cooper pressed up against her. She wanted to feel his arms around her body, touching her skin, stroking her cheek...

She wound her arms around his neck as his hands found their way to the bare skin at the small of her back. Would his fingers creep any lower? Or any higher? She wasn't quite sure which way she wanted them to go.

There was a howl from the corner of the room and they jerked apart instantly.

Baby. There was a baby in the room. She made to move towards the crib. 'Don't. I'll do it,' he said, his hands still pressed firmly against her hips.

'But you did all of last night.' She touched his shoulder. 'You're exhausted, Dan. You really should get some sleep.'

He nodded. 'And I will, as soon as you've eaten. You haven't had a chance yet. Finish breakfast, then come and take over from me.'

She eyed her toast with oodles of butter and marmalade and her steaming-hot cup of tea. How long would it take her? Five minutes? Then she could take over from Dan for a good part of the day.

From the shadows under his eyes it was clear that he needed a few hours' sleep. Could she cope with Abraham on her own for a few hours?

No matter how hard she was trying here, the thought still struck fear in her heart. What if something happened? What if she did something wrong?

The truth was she felt safer when Dan was around. Even though he told her she was doing a great job she wasn't sure she wanted to do it alone.

One of the little cardigans was hanging on the side of the crib and the solution was with her in an instant. Of course! That was what she would do. She would take Abraham upstairs to visit Mrs Van Dyke—at least then she wouldn't be on her own. And even though Mrs Van Dyke was elderly she had lots of experience with babies. She might even be able to give Carrie some tips.

She looked over to the sofa. Dan was already taking the bottle out of Abraham's mouth. He was feeding really quickly. A thought crossed her mind. 'Is your internet working yet?'

Dan shrugged his shoulders. He was deep in concentration. 'Haven't checked yet. Why?'

'Do you think there's any way we could weigh Abraham? Maybe we aren't giving him enough milk. He always seems to gulp really quickly then gets lots of wind.'

The news anchor was telling the same story over and over again. Wasn't she wearing that same suit jacket a few days ago? Pictures filled the screen of stranded cars, a collapsed tree in Central Park, aerial shots of all the roads completely covered in snow. More pictures of people being rescued by police and, in some cases, helicopters. It looked as if there had been barely any improvements in the past two days. Her voice was starting to annoy Carrie.

'Snow ploughs cleared most of New York State Thruway the I-87 this morning, only for the hard work to be destroyed less than three

hours later after another record deluge of snow. Some people had been waiting two days to get their cars out of the snowdrifts, only to get snowed back in a few miles down the thruway. Emergency services can't give an estimate on how much longer it will take to clear the thruway again. They are stressing that people in the area should only travel in emergency cases. Every resource possible is currently being used to try and restore the fluctuating power supplies to the city. Some areas of the city have been without power for more than twenty-four hours. Authorities assure us that all power supplies should be connected in the next twelve hours.'

Dan pointed at the screen. 'That's the bad news. Now wait for it—here comes the good news story.'

Carrie turned back to the screen. She definitely had seen that jacket before. Wardrobe at the news station must be as closed down as the rest of New York.

'And finally, community kitchens are springing up all over New York City. The latest is in Manhattan's Lower East Side at Sara D. Roosevelt Park and the locals have been enjoying the opportunity to gather somewhere with some hot food and heating.' The camera shot to children building a giant snowman in the park and

several residents holding cups with something steaming hot inside.

'Wow, that snowman is enormous. There's no way a kid made that. They couldn't reach that high.'

'Do I sense a little snowman envy?' Dan had an amused expression on his face.

Carrie shrugged. 'Maybe. Can't even tell you the last time I made a snowman. I must have been around ten. Back home in London I don't even have a garden.'

Dan headed over to the back window, juggling Abraham in his arms. It was time for winding again. 'Most of the apartments around here don't have gardens. But there are gardens. Have you managed to get to Washington Square Park yet?'

She joined him at the window, looking out over the snow-covered back alley. 'If I even thought we'd have a chance of making it there I'd ask you to take me.' She reached over and touched Abraham's little hand. 'But we pretty much can't take this little guy anywhere with no proper clothes, jacket or snowsuit. I guess that means we're stranded.'

It was the wrong thing to say. Almost as soon as she said the words she wanted to pull them back. She could instantly see Dan's back and shoulders stiffen, the atmosphere changing around them in a second.

'I guess the actions of others impact on us all.'

She was still touching Abraham's hand, letting his little fingers connect with hers. 'We don't know, Dan. We don't know anything.'

He spun around to face her. 'Of course we do. Look at him. Look at this defenceless little baby. Left out in the cold with hardly any clothes. He could have died out there, Carrie. He could have died.'

'Don't. Don't say that. I don't even want to think about that. I can't think about that.'

She stared him down. He had to know how much his words impacted on her. How she couldn't even bear to think the thoughts he was putting in her head.

'Why are you so critical, Dan? You must see a whole host of things in your line of work. I thought that would make you more sympathetic to people out there. Not sit as judge and master.'

'I don't judge.' His words were snapped and Abraham flinched at the rise in his voice.

'Well, I think you do. I think that's what you've done since the second I found Abraham and brought him to you.'

He opened his mouth, obviously ready to hit her with a torrent of abuse. But good sense waylaid him. She could almost see him biting his tongue and it annoyed her. She didn't want Dan to hide things from her. He should tell her how he really felt. It didn't matter that they would disagree.

'Spit it out, Dan.'

'I don't think that's wise.' His words were growled through clenched teeth.

She walked right up to him, her face directly under his chin. He was angry. She could tell he was angry. But she wasn't intimidated at all. Dan would never direct his anger at her.

'So, you can kiss me to death, but you can't tell me how you feel?'

Dan walked over to the crib, placed Abraham down and raked his hand through his short hair, his hand coming around and scraping at the bristles on his chin. 'Just leave it, Carrie.'

'Why? Isn't it normal to disagree about things? I just can't understand why the guy who was prepared to risk his life for a bunch of strangers can't take a minute to show a little compassion to a woman who is clearly desperate.' She pointed over at the crib. 'No woman in her right mind would abandon her baby. Not without good reason. I bet she's lying crying and terrified right now. I bet the past two nights she hasn't slept a wink with worry over how her son is doing.'

He shook his head. 'You're wrong, Carrie. You're more than wrong. Good people don't do things like this. Good people don't abandon their babies or make them suffer. Everyone who has the responsibility for children should put their needs first—before their own.'

She wrinkled her brow. 'What are you getting at, Dan? What need do you think Abraham's mother was putting first?'

He couldn't meet her eyes. He couldn't look at her. His eyes were fixed either on the floor or the ceiling. He walked towards the window, staring out at the snow-covered street, his hands on his hips. 'Drugs, Carrie. I think his mother was looking for her next fix.'

Carrie's hand flew up to her mouth. It hadn't even occurred to her. It hadn't even crossed her mind.

Maybe she was too innocent. Maybe she'd lived a sheltered life.

'No.' She crossed quickly to the crib and looked down at Abraham. His eyelids were fluttering, as if he was trying to focus on the changing shapes around him. He looked so innocent. So peaceful. The thought of his mother being a drug user horrified Carrie.

She hadn't lived her life in a plastic bubble. There had been women who clearly had drug problems in the maternity unit next to her's. But they were in the unit, being monitored for the sake of their babies. Although they had other issues in their lives, their babies' health was still important to them.

She reached out and stroked Abraham's skin. It still had the slightest touch of yellow, but these things wouldn't disappear overnight. Could his mother really have been taking drugs? It was just unimaginable to Carrie.

She felt a little surge of adrenalin rise inside her. 'No, Dan. No way. It can't be that. It just can't be. We would know. Abraham would be showing signs. Drug addicts' babies show signs of withdrawal, don't they? If Abraham's mother was an addict he would be screaming by now.'

'Hasn't he screamed the past two nights?'

She shook her head firmly. It didn't matter that she was no expert. She'd heard enough to know a little of the background. 'He would be sick, Dan. He would be *really* sick. And Abraham's not. Look at him.' She walked around to the other side of the crib to give Dan a clear view. 'He's not sick like that. Sure, he gets hungry and has wind. He pulls his little knees up to his chest. That's colic. Nothing else. And there are pages and pages on the internet about that.' She folded her arms across her chest. 'If we had a baby in withdrawal right now, we'd need

Shana to airlift him to the hospital. There's no two ways about it.'

It was clear from the tight expression on Dan's face that he wasn't ready to concede. He wasn't ready to consider he was wrong.

She could feel her hackles rising. She could feel they were on the precipice of a major argument and she just didn't want to go there. All her protective vibes were coming out, standing over Abraham like some lioness guarding her cub. But why would she have to guard him against Dan? The man who'd opened his door and welcomed them both in?

She took a deep breath. 'Dan, you're tired and you're cranky. I know what that feels like. Let's leave this. Go and sleep for a few hours. I'm going to take Abraham upstairs to see Mrs Van Dyke. She'll be happy to see him and, who knows, she might even give me some tips.'

She could see he still wanted to argue with her but fatigue was eating away at every movement he made. His shoulders were slumped, his muscular frame sagging.

'Fine. I'll go to sleep.' He stalked off towards the bedroom—the bed she'd recently vacated—before he halted and turned around. 'Mrs Van Dyke, ask her if she needs anything. Anything at all. I can phone Mr Meltzer and go back along to the shop in a few hours and get us some more supplies. We'll need things for Abraham anyhow.'

There it was. Even in his inner turmoil, the real Dan Cooper could still shine through. He was still thinking about others, still concerned about his elderly neighbour.

She picked up Abraham from the crib, tapping her finger on his button nose and smiling at him.

Just when she thought Dan had gone he appeared at her elbow, bending over and dropping a gentle kiss on Abraham's forehead.

'I'm not going to let anything happen to this little guy, Carrie. Nothing at all.' His words were whispered, but firm, and he turned and walked off to the bedroom, closing the door behind him.

CHAPTER NINE

CARRIE WALKED UP the stairs slowly, Abraham cradled in her arms.

The way that Dan had come over and kissed him had almost undone her. She was ready to fight with him, to argue with him over his unforgiving point of view.

But Daniel Cooper was a good guy—his most recent action only proved that. There was so much more to this than she could see. Maybe she'd been so wrapped up in her own grief and struggling with her own ability to cope with the situation that she'd totally missed something with Dan.

It just didn't figure for a warm-hearted Everyman hero to have such black-and-white views. To be so blinkered. Maybe it was time for her to crawl out of the sandbox and get back in the playground—to start to consider those around her.

She reached Mrs Van Dyke's door and gave a little knock. 'Mrs Van Dyke? It's Carrie from across the hall. May I come in?'

She heard the faint shout from the other side of the door, once again almost drowned out by the theme tune of *Diagnosis Murder*. She turned the handle and walked in, crossing the room and kneeling next to Mrs Van Dyke's brown leather armchair.

She adjusted Abraham from her shoulder, laying him between her hands so Mrs Van Dyke could have a clear look at him. 'Guess who I brought to visit,' she said quietly.

Mrs Van Dyke reached out for the remote control and silenced the television. 'Well, who do we have here?' she asked, one frail finger reaching out and tracing down the side of Abraham's cheek.

'We call him Abraham. It's been three days now and there's still no sign of his mother.'

'May I?' Mrs Van Dyke held out her thin arms. For a second Carrie hesitated, instant protective waves flooding through her, wondering about the steadiness of Mrs Van Dyke's hands. But she pushed the thoughts from her mind. This woman had held more babies, more little lives in her hands than Carrie probably would in this lifetime. She had a wealth of experience to which Carrie really needed even the tiniest exposure.

She placed Abraham in her shaky hands and watched as Mrs Van Dyke repositioned him on her lap, with her hand gently supporting his head as she leaned over and spoke to him quietly, all the while stroking one cheek with her bent finger.

It was magical. Even though Mrs Van Dyke was obviously feeling the effects of age, from her misshapen joints to her thin frame, a new life and sparkle seemed to come into her eyes when talking to Abraham. It was as if he released a little spark of life into her.

Carrie couldn't hear what she was saying. It was as if she were having an entirely private conversation with him. His little blue eyes had opened and were watching her intensely. Could he even focus yet? Carrie wasn't sure. But the conversation brought a smile to her face.

Abraham was wearing one of the beautiful hand-knitted blue cardigans that Mrs Van Dyke had given her, along with the white crocheted shawl. The recognition made Mrs Van Dyke smile all the more as she fingered the delicate wool. They still had hardly any clothes for him and without Mrs Van Dyke's contribution Abraham would have spent most of the time wrapped in a towel.

Carrie settled onto the antique-style leather sofa. 'Dan asked me to check if you needed anything. He's hoping to give Mr Meltzer a ring and go along to the shop later. Can you give me a list of what you're running short of?'

A smile danced across Mrs Van Dyke's lips. 'He's such a good boy, my Daniel.'

She almost made it sound as if he were one of her own. 'I'm surprised he didn't come up himself.'

Carrie felt her cheeks flush. She wasn't quite sure what to say. 'He's really tired. Abraham kept him awake most of the night. I told him to get some sleep and I would come up and see you.' It almost made them sound like some old married couple. She was hoping that would pass Mrs Van Dyke by.

But the old lady was far too wily for that. The smile remained on her lips and as she regarded Carrie carefully with her pale grey eyes it was almost as if she were sizing up her suitability. 'I could do with some things,' she said slowly.

'No problem. What do you need?'

'Some powdered milk—there won't be any fresh milk left. And some chocolate biscuits and some tins of soup.'

'What kind of soup do you like?'

Mrs Van Dyke smiled as she played with Abraham on her lap. 'Oh, don't worry about that. Daniel knows exactly what to get me.' She eyed Carrie again. 'Sometimes I wonder what I'd do without him.'

The words seemed to drip with loyalty and devotion to Daniel. These two had known each other for most of Daniel's life. How much had they shared?

Carrie pushed the queries out of her head. She was fascinated by how content Abraham looked, how placid he was on Mrs Van Dyke's lap, with her wholehearted attention. 'You're much better at this than me. Maybe you can give me some tips.'

Mrs Van Dyke raised her head. 'Tips? Why would you need tips?'

'Because I'm not very good at this. I think he's feeding too quickly. He gets lots of wind and screams half the night.' She pointed over at his little frame. 'I've no idea what he weighs. So I don't know if we're giving him enough milk or not. This baby stuff is all so confusing.'

Mrs Van Dyke gave her a gentle smile as Abraham wrapped his tiny fingers around her gnarled one. 'I'm sure you're much better at this than you think you are. He's around six pounds,' she said.

'How do you know that?' Carrie asked in wonder.

Mrs Van Dyke smiled. 'I just do. Years of experience. I think he might have been a few weeks early.' She touched his face again. 'But his jaundice will settle in a few days. Have you been putting him next to the window, letting the daylight get to him?'

Carrie nodded. 'Dan has a friend who is a paediatrician at Angel's Hospital. She told us what to do. I just wish we could actually get him there so he could be checked over.'

'He doesn't need to be checked. He's fine. As for the wind—he's a new baby. It will settle.' She slid her hands under his arms and sat him upright. 'It's a big adjustment being out in the big bad world. A few days ago he was in a dark cocoon, being fed and looked after. Now he's got to learn to do it for himself.'

Carrie felt a prickle of unease. 'I wish Dan felt like that.'

Mrs Van Dyke's eyes were on her in a flash. 'Felt like what?' There was the tiniest sharp edge to her voice. A protective element. Just like the way Carrie felt towards Abraham. It heightened Carrie's awareness. Mrs Van Dyke had known Daniel since he was a child. What else did she know?

Carrie gave a sigh. 'Dan doesn't think that

Abraham's mother cared about him at all. He doesn't think she looked after him. He thinks she might have been a drug user.'

She could see Mrs Van Dyke's shoulders stiffen and straighten slightly. Maybe she was wrong to use the drug word around someone so elderly.

But Mrs Van Dyke just shook her head. 'No.' Her eyes were focused entirely on Abraham. 'His mother wasn't a drug user.'

Carrie leaned back against the leather sofa. Even though it looked ancient, it was firm and comfortable. Much more comfortable than Dan's modern one. How many people had rested on this sofa over the years, laid their hands on the slightly worn armrests and heard the pearls of wisdom from Mrs Van Dyke?

'Then what happened?' She gave a sigh. 'I just can't get my head around it. I keep thinking of all the reasons in the world that would make you give up your baby, and none of them are good enough. None of them come even close. I keep thinking of alternatives—all reasons a mum could keep her baby. None of them lead to this.'

'Not every woman will have the life that you've had, Carrie.' The words were quiet, almost whispered and spoken with years of experience. The intensity of them brought an unexpected flood of tears to Carrie's eyes.

Her voice wavered. 'You say that as if I've lived a charmed life.'

'Haven't you?'

She shook her head firmly. 'I don't think so. Last year I lost my daughter. I had a stillbirth.' She looked over at Abraham, her voice still wavering. 'I came to New York to get away from babies to get away from the memories.'

Mrs Van Dyke was silent for a few moments. Maybe Carrie had stunned her with her news, but, in truth, Mrs Van Dyke didn't look as if anyone would have the capability of stunning her.

Her answer was measured. 'It seems as if we've shared the heartache of the loss of a child. At least with Peter, I had a chance to get to know him a little. To get to share a little part of his life. I'm sorry you didn't get that opportunity, Carrie.'

The sincerity in her words was clear. She meant every single one of them. And even though Carrie didn't know her well, it gave her more comfort than she'd had in a long time. Maybe this was all on her. She'd kept so much bottled up inside for so long. She didn't want to share. And now, in New York, the only two people she'd shared with had shown her sincerity and compassion—even though they were virtual strangers.

'You had five children, didn't you?'

Mrs Van Dyke nodded. 'Peter was my youngest. David, Ronald, Anne and Lisbeth all have families of their own now.'

'Are any of them still in New York?'

There was a sadness in Mrs Van Dyke's eyes. 'Sadly, no. David's in Boston. Ronald's in Washington. Lisbeth married a lovely Dutch man and is back in Holland. Anne found herself a cowboy and lives on a ranch in Texas. She spends most of her time trying to persuade me to go and live with her and her family.' Mrs Van Dyke showed some pride in her eyes. 'She has a beautiful home—a beautiful family. But I find Texas far too hot. I visit. Daniel takes me to the airport and I go and stay with Anne for part of the winter. But New York is home to me now. It always will be.' She hesitated for a moment, before looking at Carrie with her pale grey eyes. 'And Peter's here, of course. I would never leave my son.'

It was as if a million tiny caterpillars decided to run over her skin. Tiny light pinpricks all over.

Ruby. Her tiny white remembrance plaque in a cemetery in London. She'd visited it the day she left and wondered if anyone would put flowers there while she was gone. The chances were unlikely. Most people had moved on.

Part of her felt sympathy for Mrs Van Dyke not wanting to leave her beloved son. Should she feel guilty for coming to New York? All she felt was sad. Ruby wasn't there any more. Her talismans were in the box upstairs and in her heart—not on the little white plaque next to hundreds of others.

She was trying to put things into perspective. Her past situation and the current one. Trying to find a reason for Abraham's mother's behaviour.

Mrs Van Dyke's voice cut through her thoughts. 'You have to remember, Carrie. Our children belong to God. We're only given them on loan from heaven. Sometimes God calls them home sooner than we expected.'

The words of the wise. A woman who'd had years to get over the death of her young son, but it was clearly still as raw today as it had been at the time. But here she was, with the help of her faith, rationalising the world around her. Getting some comfort from it.

Carrie moved from the sofa and knelt on the ground next to Mrs Van Dyke's armchair. 'Then why would we waste any of that precious time? Why would we want to miss out on the first feed, the first smile? It's all far too precious, far too fleeting to give it up so easily. I can't believe that Abraham's mother doesn't care. I can't believe she abandoned him without a second thought.'

'It's a sad world, Carrie. But sometimes we have to realise that not everyone has the same moral standing and beliefs that you and I have. Not everyone values babies and children the way that they should.'

It was a complete turnaround. The absolute opposite of what she'd expected Mrs Van Dyke to say. But as she watched the elderly face, she realised Mrs Van Dyke was lost—stuck in a memory someplace. She wasn't talking about the here and now; she was remembering something from long ago.

It sent a horrible, uncomfortable feeling down her spine. She'd seen the awful newscasts about abused and battered children. She'd seen the adverts for foster carers for children whose parents didn't want them any more. The last thing she wanted was for Abraham to end up in any of those categories. It was just unthinkable.

She was staring at him again. Transfixed by his beautiful skin and blinking blue eyes. 'I just can't think of him like that. I just have the oddest feeling—' she put her hand on her heart '—right here, that I'm right about him. I can't explain it, but I just think that Abraham's mother didn't abandon him because she didn't love him. I think it's just the opposite. She abandoned him because she *did* love him.'

Mrs Van Dyke sat back in her chair, cradling Abraham in her arms. Carrie was almost envious of her years of experience. The strength she had to draw on. It radiated from her. Being around Mrs Van Dyke was like being enveloped in some warm, knowledgeable blanket. She could only hope that one day she would be like that, too.

After a few moments she eventually spoke. 'It seems to me like it's time to ask some hard questions, Carrie.'

The words made her a little uncomfortable. Could Mrs Van Dyke read her thoughts? See all the things that were floating around her brain about Daniel? That would really make her cheeks flush, because some of those thoughts were X-rated.

But surely Mrs Van Dyke had no inkling that anything had happened between them. She hadn't even seen them together. She couldn't possibly know.

'What kind of questions?' she finally asked.

'The kind of questions you're skirting around about. Why exactly would a mother leave a baby on our doorstep? What reasons could she possibly have? And why this doorstep? Why not another?'

Carrie sat back in her chair. All the things that had been circling in her brain for the past few days. Even though they were in the background, she hadn't really focused on them, or given them the attention they deserved. Looking after Abraham, and trying to decipher her emotions towards Daniel, had taken up all her time and energy.

It was time to sit back and take a deep breath. To look at things from a new angle, a new perspective.

'I guess I need to take some time to think about this,' she said quietly.

'I guess you do.'

It was like being in the presence of an all-knowing seer. A person who knew what was happening but left you to find it out for yourself.

She stood up and walked over to pick up Abraham again. Just holding him close seemed to give her comfort. It was amazing how quickly she was becoming attached to this tiny person.

'I'll get Dan to bring your shopping up later.'

'That's perfect, Carrie.' She gave a little nod of her head. 'You've taken on a big job, and I commend you for it. But Abraham is someone else's baby. It's so easy to love them, and it's so hard to let them go. You need to protect yourself. You need to look after your own heart.'

Carrie placed her hand across Abraham's back. 'I know that. I know that this won't last. As soon as the snow clears, Abraham will go to Angel's to be assessed. Social services already know about him. I'm sure they will already have somewhere for him to go.'

She nodded towards the television. The title for a new episode of *Diagnosis Murder* was just beginning to roll. 'I'll let you get back to your television.' Had she really been up here for an hour? 'Thank you for letting us visit, Mrs Van Dyke.'

'No, thank *you,* Carrie. I hope I'll be seeing you again soon.'

'I hope so, too.'

She headed towards the door. Even before she opened it Abraham twitched in her arms as Mrs Van Dyke reached for the remote control and the sound boomed around the apartment again.

Carrie smiled as she closed the door behind her.

She lifted her head. It was as if her own doorway was beckoning from across the hall. She'd barely been in there for the past few days. Just twice for a shower, a change of clothes or to pick up some baking ingredients.

Last time she'd been in there Dan had kissed her.

After this morning that almost seemed like a lifetime ago.

She propped Abraham up on her shoulder. She knew exactly what she was going to do now. She wanted to leave Dan to sleep a little longer. Hopefully then he would be in the mood to talk.

In the meantime she and Abraham would have some quiet time together. It didn't feel like a betrayal to have him in her arms any more. It just felt right. As if he belonged there.

But most importantly she had someone she wanted him to meet. Someone she wanted to talk to him about.

To let him know that there was room in her heart for everyone.

CHAPTER TEN

THREE HOURS LATER she was back downstairs. Abraham had slept for a few hours while she sat quietly and looked through the things in Ruby's box.

It was the first time she'd ever managed to do it without breaking her heart. She was still sad, a few tears had still slid down her cheeks. But this time it hadn't been so hard to put the things back in the box. It hadn't felt as if her life was over. It hadn't felt as if there was nothing to fight for any more.

And that wasn't just because Abraham was in her arms. It was because she was beginning to feel different.

Daniel appeared in the doorway, his hair rumpled and sticking up in every direction but the right one. 'Hey, how long did I sleep?'

She glanced at her watch. 'We've been gone for four hours. We had to come back down because Abraham needed another bottle.' She hesitated for a second. 'We need some more supplies, and Mrs Van Dyke needs some things. How would you feel about leaving Abraham with her for a little while?'

He nodded and rubbed the sleep out of his eyes. 'I think that sounds like a plan.'

'Are we almost out of nappies already?'

Dan looked over and nodded, staring into the bottom of the powdered-milk can. 'We're almost out of everything. I definitely need to buy some more coffee. It's the only thing that keeps me awake. I'm usually never this tired.'

Carrie walked over to him, leaving Abraham to kick his legs freely on the towel for a few minutes. 'You're usually never looking after a baby. How do you do on night shifts?'

He gave her a rueful look. 'The busy nights are fine. The quiet nights? I drink about six cups.'

'Will Mr Meltzer have anything left?'

Dan shook his head. 'No. We'll need to go further afield. Do you have rain boots?'

'Wellies? Sure I do.'

'Then get them. Go and get changed and I'll make a few calls to see where we can get some supplies. Are you okay walking a few blocks?'

'Of course. Do you want me to take Abraham up to Mrs Van Dyke?'

He shook his head. 'No, I'll do it. You go and get changed.'

She should have known. Dan wanted to check on Mrs Van Dyke himself. He really was a good guy. So why was he so down on Abraham's mother? It just didn't fit with the rest of his demeanour.

Ten minutes later she was ready. Her pink wool coat, purple scarf and purple woolly hat pulled down over her ears. Her wellies firmly in place with her jeans tucked inside.

The nip of frost was still in the air as they stepped outside. Dan pushed a piece of paper into his pocket and held out his gloved hand towards her.

Carrie hesitated for just a second. There was nothing in this. He was being mannerly and making sure she didn't fall over in the snow. This wasn't about the kiss that they'd shared—not at all.

She put her hand in his. 'How far do we need to go?'

The snow was deeper than she'd expected. Not quite deep enough to reach the tops of her wellies, but not too far off it. 'A few blocks,' he murmured.

It only took a few minutes for her to realise that trudging through the snow was harder work than she first thought. She could feel her cheeks flush and her breathing get harder. This was the most exercise she'd had in days. But there was something almost magical about being the first set of footprints in the clean, bright snow.

They walked for ten minutes before they came across their first snowman. He was built in the middle of the sidewalk at a peculiar angle. The hat had slipped and one of the stones that had been an eye had fallen out.

Dan smiled as she stopped to admire him. 'Oh, no. Here she goes. Snowman envy again.'

'What do you mean?'

'I saw your face when you watched the news report. The shops we're visiting are right next to Washington Square Park. If you really want we could stop and build one.'

She shook her head. 'But I didn't bring a carrot. Every good snowman needs a carrot for a nose.' She smiled. 'Actually, I'd much prefer to do a snow angel. Less work, more fun.'

They walked around the edge of the park towards the shops. There were a number of independent stores with lights on inside. Dan pushed open one of the doors quickly and shouted through to the back. 'Aidan, are you there?'

'Hi, Dan.' The guy appeared quickly from the back of the shop. 'Sorry, the phone keeps going ever since I got here. Seems the whole world needs supplies right now.' He nodded to the bags on the counter. 'I think I've got everything you requested—including the baby supplies. Anything you want to tell me, buddy?'

He looked from Dan to Carrie, and back again. 'It's not what you think. We found a baby on our doorstep a few days ago. Social services can't get through to pick him up and we need some supplies to take care of him.'

Dan's face was a bit flushed. As if he knew exactly what Aidan had been thinking. Was he embarrassed? Was he embarrassed that people might think they were actually a couple?

'This is my neighbour Carrie. She's giving me a hand with the baby.'

It seemed so.

Aidan nodded at Carrie and rang up the purchases on the register. 'Hopefully this will last only another day or so. Then you'll both be able to stop playing babysitter.'

The phone started ringing again and he headed back through to the back of the store. Dan had picked up the bags from the counter but seemed frozen. A bit like Carrie.

Another day or so. Abraham would be gone in a matter of days—maybe hours. What would happen to him then? Would he just get lost in the New York care system and be handed out to a foster family? The thought made Carrie feel sick. Before she'd been worried about Dan being embarrassed by her. Now, she realised she had much more to worry about.

She was going to have to say goodbye to another baby.

They walked out into the clear day. The snow was still thick everywhere, but the sky was clear and bright. Maybe this was the beginning of the end of the bad weather. Maybe it was time to move forward.

Dan seemed as lost in his thoughts as Carrie. Was he thinking about Abraham, too, or was he thinking about her?

They reached the edge of the park, near the Washington Arch. There were a few figures dotted around the park and a whole host of snowmen. 'Look.' Carrie pointed. 'It's like a whole little family.' She stood next to the father snowman and looked down at the carefully erected snow family. 'Dad, mum, a son and a daughter. How cute.' Her voice had a wistful tone that she couldn't help. Even the snow people had happy families.

Dan lifted his eyebrows at her. 'Snow angels?' he asked.

She wanted him to say so much more. She wanted to know how he was feeling. But Dan just wouldn't reveal that side of himself to her.

In a way he was even more closed off to her than Mark had been.

She gave a little nod. 'Snow angels.' This could be the last thing they would do together. She might as well have a little fun.

They found a bit of untouched ground. 'It's perfect,' said Carrie. 'Are you ready?'

She walked as gingerly as she could in her wellies and turned around holding her hands open wide. Dan left the bags on the ground and stood next to her, hands wide, their fingers almost touching. 'You do realise you're about to get soaked, right, Brit girl?'

'It's a question of whether I care or not,' she responded as she leaned backwards, arms wide, letting herself disappear in a puff of powdery snow. She waved her hands through the snow as fast as she could, laughing, as Dan tried to keep up with her. Snow was soaking through her coat quickly, edging in around her neck and up her coat sleeves.

Then she felt it, her fingers brushing his, and she stopped.

She turned her head to face his. All of a sudden it seemed as if they were the only two people in New York. The only two people in this park, in this universe.

Dan moved. His breathing just as quick as hers. The warm air spilling into the cold around him, and then he was on her. His legs on either side of her, his warm breath colliding with her own.

'What are you doing to me, Carrie McKenzie?' His brown eyes were full of confusion and it made her heart squeeze. There it was. For the first time. Daniel Cooper stripped bare.

'What are you doing to me, Daniel Cooper? I thought I was doing fine till I met you.'

She pushed her neck up, catching his cold lips with hers. Wrapping her hands around his neck and pulling him even closer. She didn't mind the cold snow seeping through her coat around her shoulders and hips. She pushed aside the fact that a few minutes ago she'd felt a little hurt when he'd introduced her as his neighbour. She was as confused about all this as he was.

She'd told him everything. She'd told him about Ruby. She'd told him about Mark. But how much did she know about Daniel Cooper? And why did she feel as if she'd only scraped the surface?

In a few days the snow would be cleared, Abraham would be gone and their lives would return to normal. But what was normal any more? What would happen to her and Dan? An occasional hello on the stairs? She couldn't bear that.

He pulled away and stood up, holding out his hands to pull her up from the snow. 'Let's go, Carrie. You'll catch your death out here.'

The moment was past. It was over. Just as they would soon be.

She swallowed the lump in her throat. Now the wet patches were starting to feel uncomfortable. Starting to make her notice the cold air around them.

'I guess it's time to get back,' she said quietly.

'I guess it is.' He picked up the bags and started towards the exit, leaving her feeling as if she'd just imagined their kiss.

Two hours later, dried off and with clean clothes, Carrie finished making coffee for Dan and tea for herself, before adding the fruit scones that she'd made upstairs to a plate. Baby Abraham was in a good mood and feeding happily after being picked up from Mrs Van Dyke's.

Dan grinned at her. 'I wondered what the smell was. Do you know it drifted down the stairs and woke me up earlier? Not that I'm complaining.'

'Butter and raspberry jam. I hope you like them.'

'I'm sure I will.' He held her gaze for a minute and it made her wonder what he was thinking about. Was he regretting having her help with Abraham? Because she wasn't regretting it for a second.

'What did you do when I was sleeping—apart from baking?'

'I went upstairs and visited with Mrs Van Dyke. She's lovely—really lovely. Abraham seemed to like her, too.'

'Everybody likes her. She's just one of those people.'

'Was she good friends with your grandmother?'

Dan nodded. 'They lived in the same apartment block for sixty years and spoke to each other every day. Things were a bit different in those days—they used to borrow from each other all the time. There was hardly a day that went by where my grandmother didn't send me up the stairs to borrow or return something.'

'Did you meet her family?'

Dan adjusted himself in the seat as he fed Abraham. He looked slightly uncomfortable. 'They were all a good bit older than me.'

'The same age as your mother?' She couldn't help it. Both of them were tiptoeing around the issue. She didn't want to ask him about his mother, and he hadn't volunteered any information.

'Yeah, around about the same age.'

Nothing else. It was his prime opportunity

to tell her a little more and he hadn't taken it. Should she give up? Maybe some things were best left secret. But it just felt so strange.

She took a deep breath.

'How come you ended up staying with your grandmother? Was your mum sick?'

Dan let out a laugh, causing Abraham to startle in his arms. But it wasn't a happy laugh. It was one filled with anger and resentment. 'Oh, yeah, she was sick all right.'

'What does that mean?'

'It means that some people shouldn't be mothers, Carrie.'

He didn't hesitate with his words and it made the breath catch in her throat.

What did that mean? Was that just aimed at his mother? Or was it aimed at her, too?

Was this why he was so screwed up about Abraham? He thought Abraham's mother wasn't fit to have a child?

'Is your mother still alive, Dan?' It seemed the natural question.

'No.' His words were curt and sharp. 'She died ten years ago. Drug overdose.'

The words were a shock and not what she was expecting to hear. Lots of people she knew had lost their mum or dad to various illnesses, cancer or some tragic accident. But no one had ever had a parent die from a drug overdose.

One boy that Carrie had gone to school with had died a few years ago from drugs, but that was the only person she knew.

Chills were flooding over her body. Dan's reactions were acidic, obviously affected by years of bitter experience. What kind of a relationship had he had with his mother? It couldn't have been good.

'I'm sorry, Dan. I'm sorry that your mother died of a drug overdose. That must have been awful for you.'

He stood up as Abraham finished his bottle and propped him up onto his shoulder. 'It wasn't awful at all. I hadn't seen her in years. Nor did I want to.'

Carrie was at a loss. Should she ask more questions or just stay quiet? There was that horrible choice between seeming nosey or seeming uninterested. The last thing she wanted to do was upset Dan—he'd been so good to her. But she also wanted to support him as much as he'd supported her. Surely there was something she could do.

And then she remembered. His touch, and how much it had meant to her.

She walked over and laid her hand on his arm. His eyes went to her hand, just for a second, then lifted to meet her eyes.

She could see the hesitation, the wariness in

them. He'd revealed a little part of himself, but there was so much more. She'd shared the most important part of her. It had hurt. It had felt as if she were exposing herself to the world. Taking her heart right out of her body and leaving it for the world to spear.

And what hurt most here was that Dan didn't feel ready or able to share with her. Had she totally misread the situation? She'd thought they had connected. She thought that there might even have been a chance of something more. But if Dan couldn't share with her now, how on earth could they go any further?

The television flashed in the background. Pictures of snow being cleared in some areas, with aerial shots of previously deserted streets now with a few people on them, or a single car slowly edging its way along. The snow was finally going to stop. New York was going to return to a sense of normality.

Maybe it was for the best. Abraham would be able to go to Angel's Hospital and be checked over by Shana. That was good, except it made her want to run over and snatch him out of Dan's arms.

How much longer would she be able to cuddle him? Would this be their last night together? And what hurt more, the thought of being separated from Abraham, or the thought of not having a reason to spend time with Dan any more?

It was almost as if Abraham sensed her discomfort. He chose that precise moment to pull his little legs up, let out a squeal and projectile vomit all over Dan's shoulder.

Her reactions were instant. She held out her arms to take Abraham from him.

'Yeuch!' Dan pulled his T-shirt over his head, trying to stop the icky baby sick from soaking through. It was an almost unconscious act and she tried not to be distracted by his flat abdomen and obvious pecs. If only her stomach looked like that.

But it didn't—ever. No matter what the TV ads said, women's abdomens just weren't designed to look like that, even *before* they'd had a baby.

Stifling a sigh, she pretended to fuss over Abraham as Daniel walked past on his way to the laundry basket. What about his shoulders? And his back? Was the view from behind just as good?

She tried to take a surreptitious glance and her breath caught in her throat. While Daniel's torso was something a model would be envious of—his back was entirely different.

Scars. Chicken-pox scars all across his back. She winced inwardly, remembering how itchy she'd been as a child when she was covered with the spots. She'd only had a few on her back and they'd driven her insane because she couldn't—probably thankfully—get to them to scratch them.

'This is my favourite T-shirt,' he moaned as he flung it into the laundry basket. 'I bet no matter what I use, I'll never get rid of that smell.'

He looked up and caught sight of her face. She felt her cheeks flush and looked down at Abraham again.

But it was too late. He'd seen the expression that she'd tried to hide. He'd seen the shock. And maybe a little bit of horror.

She wanted to take back the past few seconds. She wanted to stand here with a smile fixed on her face. But it was too late.

Dan made to walk past, heading to his bedroom to get another T-shirt and cover up, the shadows apparent in his eyes. But something made her act. She put Abraham down in the crib and grabbed Dan's arm on the way past.

'What?' he snapped.

'Stop, Dan. Just stop for a second.'

She had no medical background. She had no training whatsoever. But something had registered in her brain. Something inside was screaming at her.

She nervously reached her fingers up and touched his back. He flinched, obviously annoyed at her touch. His voice was lower. 'What are you doing, Carrie?'

Her fingers were trembling. She was almost scared to touch his flesh. But something was wrong. Something was very wrong.

The scars weren't what she'd expected. She had chicken-pox scars herself. And she and her fellow friends had spent many teenage years debating over how to hide their various scars.

Chicken-pox scars were pitted and uneven. No two looked the same.

But that wasn't the case on Dan's back. All his scars looked the same. Uniformly pitted circles across his back with not a single one on his chest, arms or face. Nothing about this was right.

Her pinkie fitted inside the little uniform scars. They were all the same diameter, all perfect scars, but of differing depth. Almost as if…

'Oh, Dan.' Her hand flew to her mouth and tears sprang to her eyes. She'd seen scars like these before. But only single ones, caused by accident by foolish friends.

These hadn't been caused by accident. These had been inflicted on a little boy. One at a time. Cigarette burns. She couldn't even begin to imagine what kind of a person could do this to a child. What kind of a person could willingly and knowingly inflict this kind of pain on another human being. It was beyond unthinkable.

Everything fell into place. Dan's reactions. His feelings towards his mother. The fact he'd ended up staying with his grandmother.

She reached her hands up around his neck and pulled him towards her. 'Oh, Dan, I'm so sorry. Your mother did this to you, didn't she?'

He was frozen. Frozen to the spot at his secret being exposed.

Even as her hands had wrapped around his neck her fingers had brushed against some of the scars. It was so unfair. So cruel. It made her feel sick to her stomach.

Finally, he answered. 'Yes. Yes, she did.' She could feel the rigid tension disperse from his muscles.

He walked back over and sagged down on the sofa, Carrie at his side. She didn't want to leave him—not for a second. Carrie couldn't stop the tears that were flowing now. Tears for a damaged child. Tears for a ruined childhood.

She shook her head. 'Why? Why would she do something like that? Why would *anyone* behave like that towards a child?'

The words he spoke were detached. 'Not everyone is like you, Carrie. Not everyone is like Mrs Van Dyke or my grandmother.' The words were catching in his throat, raw with emotion. 'My mother should never have had children. I was a mistake. She never wanted me. I ruined her drug habit. As soon as her doctor knew she was pregnant my mother was put on a reducing programme—even all those years ago. She couldn't wait to get her next fix. When she didn't use, she was indifferent to me, when she did use, she was just downright nasty. My grandmother tried time and time again to get her to give me up. Most of the time my mother kept moving around the city, trying to stay out of the way of my grandmother, social services and the drug dealers she owed money to.' He ran his fingers through his hair. 'Drugs aren't a new problem in New York. They're an old one. One that affected me since before I was even born.'

His other hand was sitting on his lap and she intertwined her fingers with his.

Touch. The one thing she knew to do that felt right.

So many things were making sense to her now. So many of the words that he'd spoken, or, more importantly, not spoken. So many of his underlying beliefs and tensions became crystal clear, including his prejudices towards Abraham's mother.

She would probably feel the same herself

if she'd been in his shoes. But something still didn't sit right in her stomach about this whole situation.

She squeezed his hand. 'So how did you end up with your grandmother, then?'

'The cops phoned her. Our latest set of neighbours heard the screams once too often.' Carrie flinched. She didn't like any of the pictures her mind was currently conjuring up. 'They were concerned—but didn't want to get involved. Fortunately for me, one of their friends was a cop.'

'And he just picked you up and took you out of there?'

Dan shook his head. It was apparent he didn't like the details. 'It was more complicated than that. Social services were involved, as well as the police—it took a little time to sort out. But from the second I set eyes on the cop in my mother's house I knew I would be safe. There was just something about the guy. He wasn't leaving without me—no matter what happened.'

She gave him a smile. 'I guess he paved your way to the police academy.'

'I guess he did. He even gave me a reference eighteen years later when I needed it.'

'And what did your grandmother say?'

He shook his head. 'Nothing. Nothing at all.

My mother's name was never mentioned again. As far as I know she never had any more contact with my mother. Neither of us did. I can only ever remember a woman from social services coming to the door once. That was it. Nothing else.'

There was silence for a few seconds, as if both of them were lost in their thoughts. 'Thank you,' Carrie whispered.

'For what?' He looked confused.

'For sharing with me.'

'But I didn't. Not exactly.'

'It doesn't matter. Now I understand why you're so concerned about Abraham.'

They both turned towards the crib. 'I can't allow him to have a life like that, Carrie. If his mother didn't want him, then maybe this is the best thing for him. To go to loving parents who do want him. There are thousands of people out there who can't have kids of their own, just waiting for a baby like Abraham.'

Carrie hesitated. She didn't want to upset him. What he said made sense, but it still just didn't ring true with her.

'I get that, Daniel. I do. But I still think there's something else—something that we're both missing here.'

'Like what?'

She stood up and walked over to the window.

The newscaster had been right. She could see the difference in the snow outside. It wasn't quite so deep. It wasn't quite so white. No freshly lain snow was replacing its supplies and what was there was beginning to disintegrate, to turn to the grey slush that had been on the streets before.

This time tomorrow Abraham would be gone. Gone forever. And the thought made her heart break.

She turned to face him again, her arms folded across her chest. 'Why here, Dan? Why this house? There are plenty of nice houses on this street. What made Abraham's mother leave him *here?*' She pointed downwards, emphasising her words.

Daniel lifted his hands. 'What do you mean, Carrie? We've been through this. The lights were on. This place was a safe bet. Even if the mother didn't ring the bell.'

'That's it.' She was across the room in a flash, a little light going on in her brain. 'A safe bet. Don't you get it?' She grabbed hold of his arms.

'Get what?'

Her frustration was mounting. 'Dan, I knew you were a cop—even though you'd never spoken to me. I saw you every day in your uniform.

Walking along this street and into our apartment building.'

'So?' A wrinkle appeared on his brow.

'So!' Her face was inches from his. The compassion in her eyes more prominent than anything he'd ever seen. 'What's a safer bet than a cop? If you had to leave a baby at anyone's door, who would you choose, Dan? Who would you choose?'

A horrible feeling of realisation started to wash over his skin. A horrible feeling that he'd missed something really important.

'You think the baby was left here because someone knew I was a cop?'

'I *know* he was. Think about it, Dan. It makes perfect sense. If I wanted to keep my baby safe—and couldn't tell anyone about it—where safer than at a cop's door.'

'But who? Who would do something like that?'

Their eyes met. It was as if a mutual thought had just appeared in their heads. One that left a sinking feeling in his stomach. But Carrie wasn't about to stand back and leave things unsaid. Leave possibilities unchallenged.

She looked at Abraham again and tried to keep the tremble from her voice. 'Dan, is there any chance—any possibility at all—that Abraham could be your baby?'

'What? No! Of course not.' There was pain in her eyes. Hurt there for him to see. It didn't matter to her how painful the suggestion was, Abraham came first. She was thinking only of him.

It was there, in that split second, that he knew. Carrie McKenzie was the girl for him. He loved her, with his whole heart. The past few days had let deep emotions build, heartbreaking secrets revealed by both of them.

But as he looked at her flushed face, her blue eyes trying to mask the pain she didn't want him to see, her teeth biting her plump bottom lip as she tried to digest his answer, he absolutely knew. This was a woman who was prepared to push her feelings aside for a child she had no responsibility for, no connection with. If he pulled her to the side right now and told her there was a strong likelihood that Abraham was his—even though that wasn't a possibility—he knew she would just nod quietly and say nothing. All for the sake of the child.

The one thing he'd never been able to do—connect with a woman—he'd found here, in his own home and right on his doorstep. His fractured relationship with his mother had made him erect barriers even he couldn't see. But here, and now, with Carrie McKenzie, they were gone. She wasn't shying away from him because he'd been an abused child. She was only trying to understand him better.

'Are you sure?' She was struggling with the words, trying to be steady and rational even though he knew inside she wasn't.

It only took a step to reach her and touch her cheek—no, cradle her cheek in his hand. 'I promise you, Carrie. There's no chance that Abraham is mine. That's not why he's been left here.'

There were tears brimming in her eyes. Tears of relief? She let the air out of her lungs with a little whoosh. Her bottom lip was trembling and he ached to kiss her. But it wasn't the time. They were on the precipice of something here. The precipice of something for them and something for Abraham. And they both had too much duty and responsibility to know what came first.

He didn't ever want to do that to her again. He didn't ever want to do anything to cause Carrie McKenzie even a second of hurt, a second of pain. Once was enough. She was far too precious to him for that.

She looked at him with her big blue eyes, words hovering on her lips, before she broke eye contact and looked down at the floor. Anything they had to say to each other would have to wait, if just for a few hours. She lifted her head again. 'Then it must be someone else, Dan. Someone that knows you're a cop and trusts you.'

He tried to rack his brain. 'I just can't think, Carrie. Most of my friends don't stay around here. And none of them are pregnant.' He glanced towards the window again. 'And the snow might be beginning to clear now, but it was thick on Monday night. It could only have been someone around here, someone local....' His voice tailed off and he pressed his hand against the window.

'What if it isn't a friend, Dan? What if it's a neighbour? Or someone you've come into contact with because of your job? Is there anyone around here you've been called out to see?'

'I usually work in the middle of the city. I've only ever covered a few shifts down here. It doesn't do any good covering your own patch.'

'Who did you get called out to see when you visited? Anyone that sticks in your mind?'

He felt the blood rush from his head right down to his toes. He could be sick, right now, all over the floor.

He made a mad dash for the phone, pressing the numbers furiously. 'It's Daniel Cooper. I need to speak to the captain. Now!'

'Dan, what is it? What have you remembered?'

He shook his head. He didn't have time for small talk. All he could do was pray that some of the roads had cleared and help would be available if needed.'

'Captain, it's Dan. This baby? Yes, he's fine. But I think I know who put him here. Look up Mary and Frank Shankland…. Yes, that's them. A list of domestics as long as your arm. Last time I was there, she was pregnant, he was mad and he'd beat her so badly she lost the baby. Told her if she ever got pregnant again, he'd do the same.'

Carrie's hand flew to her mouth. 'Oh, no! That's awful.'

Dan lifted his hand to silence her as he listened to the other end of the phone. 'That's why she was unprepared. She couldn't buy anything for this baby or else he might notice. She must have hidden her pregnancy from him. How are the roads? Can you send a unit? I'm going there. Now.'

He slammed down the phone and headed straight for the door. 'Wait, Dan, you can't go there alone. Look at your hand—you're already injured. How will you be able to protect her with a broken wrist?'

He spun around, his eyes furious. 'I can't, no, I *won't* wait another second, Carrie. Why didn't I think of this? After what he did to Mary the last time, we'll be lucky if she's still alive.' He pointed over to the crib. 'Take care of Abraham. Take care of Abraham for his mother. And just pray I get there in time.'

And in an instant he was gone.

CHAPTER ELEVEN

IT WAS THE longest two hours of Carrie's life. Every time she heard a siren her heart was in her mouth. Every time she heard the start-up of a car engine she would run to the window to peer outside.

Abraham was perfect. He fed and winded like a little dream. It was as if he knew how stressed and on edge she was. The noise of the snow plough coming down the street nearly tipped her over the edge. Most of the snow was starting to melt and it merely ploughed the dirty slush ahead of it.

Finally, there was a flashing blue light and the sound of a door slamming. She ran and opened Dan's apartment door.

There was a scuff mark on his cheek, as if he'd hit a wall. And his clothes, although still intact, were definitely rumpled. As if someone had clutched them in a tight grip.

Behind him, a uniformed officer was lurking, obviously waiting to hear their interaction. She couldn't stop herself. With Abraham in one arm, her other was wrapped around Dan's neck in an instant. 'Are you okay? Are you hurt? What about Abraham's mother? Please tell me that she's okay?'

Dan turned and nodded to the other cop. 'Give me five minutes, Ben. I'll be right out.' It was then Carrie noticed the baby car seat in Ben's hands. He nodded at Dan, and left it sitting next to the door.

Dan closed the door and leaned against it for a few seconds, catching his breath, before finally leaning over and dropping a kiss first on Abraham's head and then on Carrie's.

He walked over to the sofa and put his head in his hands.

Her heart was breaking for him. It was obvious he was blaming himself for this. Even though it had been entirely out of his control.

She sat next to him, the length of her thigh in contact with his. Even the slightest touch gave her a little comfort. But she couldn't find the patience to wait. Two hours had been long enough. She had to know. She had to know Abraham still had a mother.

'What happened, Dan? Does Abraham belong to Mary Shankland?'

He nodded and lifted his head from his hands.

His eyes were heavy with fatigue and strain. 'It was just as I suspected. She hid the pregnancy and gave birth in secret. She knew she would have to hide him from Frank, and thought she would have made it to a women's shelter or a hospital. But everything conspired against her.' He held up his hands. 'The weather. The snow. Then Abraham came four weeks early. She was desperate. She didn't know what to do. Frank was at the pub and was due home any minute. She didn't have time to pack up the kids and leave, and they didn't have anywhere to go.' He shook his head in frustration. 'She couldn't even get through to emergency services.'

'So she left the baby here, with you?' Carrie wrinkled her nose. 'Why didn't she ring the bell? Why didn't she ask for your help?'

He thumped his hand on the table. 'She did, Carrie! She did ring the bell. My darn music was on too loud. I never heard it. Frank was due back any minute and she'd left the children by themselves. She had to get back home before he knew anything was wrong.' He turned to face her, his eyes full of sorrow. 'If you hadn't been upstairs and heard Abraham…' He was shaking his head, obviously imagining the worst.

She clutched at his hand. 'But I did, Dan. And Abraham's safe.' She took a little moment to look at the sleeping baby on her lap. Perfect.

Perfect in every way. And more importantly, safe. Something squeezed at her heart. Every baby like Abraham and every child like Dan had the right to be safe. Had the right to be cared for and loved. Had the right to be treated with respect. If only everyone in this world felt the same.

'How are Mary and the other kids?'

Dan nodded slowly, letting a long stream of air out through his pursed lips. 'She's safe now. We arrived just as Frank was kicking off. It looks as if his temper has got worse and worse over the past few days with the family being snowed in together. Mary was crouched in a corner sheltering her youngest son.' The words sent a horrible shiver down her spine.

'Oh, those poor children.'

He nodded. 'Frank's been arrested. Mary is being checked over at Grace Jordan Hospital.' He reached over and touched Abraham's tiny fingers. 'I almost couldn't persuade her to go. She wanted to come straight here and check on Abraham. It was awful, Carrie. The tears of pure relief when she saw me and knew that I was there to help. It was a look I recognised.' He shook his head again. 'I should have got there sooner. I should have known.'

'But you didn't know, Dan. *We* didn't know.'

'But you didn't let your past history cloud

your judgement—stop you from looking at other possibilities.'

'Of course I did, Dan! How many times did I tell you I couldn't do this? I couldn't look after Abraham? I couldn't help you?'

But Dan was still fixated on his own failings. 'I shouldn't even be doing this job. How can I be a good cop when I can't even think straight?'

'Stop it. Stop it right now. You're the finest cop I've ever met, Dan Cooper. You have the biggest, kindest heart in the world. You can't help what happened to you in the past. And even though you had a crummy mother with a terrible addiction, even though you experienced things a child should never experience, it's shaped you, Dan. It's made you become the fine man that you are.' She reached over and touched his cheek. 'You feel passionately about things. You have a clear sense of right and wrong. You have the courage of your convictions. You looked at the example of the cop who looked out for you and used him as your role model. Him, Dan—not your mother. He would be proud of you. I know he would. Just like your grandmother would be.' She could feel her eyes pooling with tears. 'I couldn't have got through the past few days without you.' She looked at Abraham in her lap. 'No, *we* couldn't have got through the past few days without you.'

The tension seemed to dispel from his muscles, the frustration to abate from his eyes. He reached over and cupped her cheek, brushing her curls behind her ears. 'Carrie, you know what I need to do now, don't you? I need to take Abraham to Angel's. Shana is waiting to see him. And I need to reunite him with his mother.'

Carrie could feel the pooled tears start to spill down her cheeks. Of course. This was what she'd always wanted to happen. For Abraham to be safe, to be returned to his mother. So why did it feel as if her heart were breaking?

These past few days had been hard. But they'd also been wonderful. She finally felt healed. She finally felt as if she could start to live again.

And she'd found someone she wanted to do that with.

But their cosy little bubble was about to burst. The snow was melting. Things would get back to normal. New York would get back to normal.

Dan would get back to normal. There would be no reason for them to be stuck in his apartment together. There would no reason for her to be in his life at all.

She tried to concentrate. She tried to focus.

Last thing she wanted to do was appear like a blubbing wreck.

Abraham's eyes flickered open and she leaned over him. 'Well, Abraham, it's time to say goodbye. Or maybe I should call you Baby Shankland now?' She raised her eyebrows at Dan and he shook his head and gave her a sad little smile.

'Mary loved the name. He's definitely going to stay an Abraham.'

A tiny bit of the pressure in her chest felt relieved. He wouldn't have another name. He'd have the name that they'd given him—together. At least that little part of their time together would live on, even if nothing else did.

She ran her finger lightly over his face, touching his forehead, his eyelids, his nose, his cheeks and his mouth. Trying to savour every second, trying to imprint on her brain everything about him. Something caught her eye. His little soft fontanelle, it was pulsing. She could see the proof of his heartbeat right before her eyes. She hadn't noticed it before and it gave her even more comfort than she could have imagined.

She tried not to let her voice shake. 'I'm going to wish you a long, happy and healthy life, Abraham. I'm going to tell you that you're blessed. You're blessed to have a mother who did her best to protect you. And every time I see snow I'm going to think of you and remember you here—' she pressed her hand to her chest '—in my heart. Now and always.'

She wrapped him a little tighter in Mrs Van Dyke's crocheted shawl. She was sure Mrs Van Dyke wouldn't mind it going to a good home. She couldn't even lift her head to look at Dan right now. She already knew he was holding out his hands, waiting for Abraham, to take him away.

She must have paused. She must have waited just a little too long. Because his hand touched her arm. 'Carrie.' It wasn't a question. It was a prompt, in the quietest, subtlest way.

She put one final kiss on Abraham's forehead and held him out with shaky hands. It took all her self-control not to snatch him back from Dan's grasp.

She felt his hand on her shoulder. A tight squeeze. Followed by his voice murmuring in her ear. 'I don't know how long I'll be, Carrie. I could be all night. I need to stay with Abraham at the hospital, then fill out a mountain of paperwork downtown.'

She was nodding automatically at his words. Not really taking any of them in.

Her heart was thudding in her chest. Was this it? Was this it for them, too?

Dan hadn't said anything. She had no idea what would happen next.

All she knew was she wanted him to stay. She wanted him to stay with her. She wanted him to wrap his arms around her and tell her that everything would be okay. She wanted him to reach out and tuck her hair behind her ears. She wanted him to look at her the way he had the night before, right before he'd kissed her. She wanted to feel her heartbeat quicken and flutter in her chest as it did when they were together.

Anything other than this horrible leaden feeling that was there right now.

He released his fingers on her shoulder and she heard his footsteps heading for the door.

No words. He hadn't said anything to her. He hadn't told her to stay. He hadn't told her to go.

She heard the final hesitant steps and then the click of the door behind her.

It sounded so final. It sounded like the end of everything.

And it probably was.

And then the sobs that had been stifled in her chest finally erupted.

CHAPTER TWELVE

DAN'S WHOLE BODY wanted to go into shutdown mode. But his brain was buzzing. It had been twenty-four hours since he'd slept.

The check-over at the hospital for Mary Shankland had taken much longer than expected. She had three broken ribs and a minor head injury. It had taken hours before she was cleared for transfer and Dan didn't want anyone else to have the job of reuniting her with her son.

He wouldn't have missed it for the world.

Abraham was fine and healthy. He'd even managed to squirt a little pee all over Shana, much to Dan's amusement, as she'd examined him.

But the real heart-stopping moment had been when Mary finally got to hold her baby in her arms. She sobbed and sobbed, telling him how much she loved him and how she just wanted to protect him. The hospital social worker had been standing by to help find the family alternative accommodation and to assess them. And even though Frank had been taken to jail, a temporary restraining order had been put into place to protect the family in the meantime. All of which added to the mountain of paperwork toppling over on his desk.

His captain had been as understanding as could be. But there were still professional requirements that Dan had to fulfil. Pages and pages of paperwork that had to be completed before he could leave the station and get back home to Carrie.

Back home to where he wanted to be.

Back home to the one he wanted to be with.

Things had been too hard. Taking Abraham away from Carrie had been hard, and he'd tried his best not to make it any more difficult than it already was.

There was so much to say. So much to do. He didn't have a single doubt in his head about Carrie McKenzie. But would she have any doubts about him? There was only one way to find out.

He'd made three pit stops on his way home, his stomach churning the whole way. Thankfully the New York florist he'd visited hadn't even flinched when he'd asked her for 'rose-coloured' roses. There might have been a slight glimmer of a smile while she'd walked to her back storeroom and reappeared with beautiful, rich pink-coloured roses with the tiniest hint of red, and tied them with a matching satin ribbon.

Perfect. Just like the roses his grandmother used to fill the apartment with. It was time to do that all over again.

He walked up the stairs to his apartment building with trepidation in his heart. As he pushed open the door to his apartment he already knew she wasn't there. He could feel it. Just her presence in a room made it light up.

His feet were on the stairs in an instant, thudding upstairs and knocking on the door of her apartment. The snow had started to clear, but most people hadn't returned to work yet; the subway still wasn't completely open.

Please don't be at work. Please don't be at work.

'Carrie? Are you there? It's Dan. I need to speak to you.' He waited a few seconds, then dropped to his knees and tried to peer through the keyhole.

The door behind him creaked open. Mrs Van Dyke's thin frame and loose cardigans filled the doorway. 'I think the person you're looking for is in here,' she whispered.

'She is? What's she doing?'

Mrs Van Dyke shrugged. 'It appears I need

some help with tidying up. She's in my spare room.'

He hurried inside, knowing exactly where to go. That was just like Carrie. Now that she knew about Mrs Van Dyke's hoarding she would be doing her best to try and help. He walked over to the room, hearing the muffled noises of falling cardboard boxes inside.

'Yikes!'

His heartbeat accelerated as he elbowed his way into the room, past the teetering piles and fallen boxes, finally reaching Carrie in a heap on the floor. He grasped her hand and pulled her upwards, straight into his arms.

'Dan!' She looked dazed, and it took him a few moments to steady her. Then the arms that had rested on his shoulders fell back to her sides.

'What do you want, Dan?' She sounded sad, tired even.

'I wanted to see you.'

'Why? Why did you want to see me, Dan?'

He reached up and touched her cheek. 'I wanted to speak to you. I wanted to make sure you were okay.'

Her hand reached up and covered his. 'I'm fine, Daniel. I'm just glad that Abraham is back with his mother.'

His gut was twisting. She was still hurting,

still in pain because of the whole situation he'd allowed her to become involved in.

'Abraham is fine. Mary Shankland is fine— well, not really, but she will be. But what I'm most interested in is you, Carrie. Are you fine?'

Her eyelids widened, as if she was surprised at his words.

He pulled her a little closer. 'I've been thinking about you all night and all day. I couldn't get away—I had a mountain of paperwork to fill out. I'm so sorry I had to leave you, Carrie. I know how hard it was. But I had to take Abraham back to his mother. I had to make sure they were both okay. Even though the person I wanted to be with was you.'

'It was?' Her lips were trembling. Her whole body was trembling.

'Of course it was, Carrie.'

'But you didn't say anything. You didn't ask me to stay.' She was shaking her head as if she was trying to make sense of things.

'I couldn't, Carrie. I didn't want to start a conversation with you that I couldn't finish. Not when I had things to sort out. I wanted us to have time. Time to talk. Time to see what you wanted.' He brushed her hair behind her ear and whispered, 'What do you want, Carrie? What do you want to happen now?'

She was hesitating. As if she was scared to

say the words out loud. He was praying inside it was because she was nervous and not because she wanted to let him down gently.

He lifted up the hand-tied bouquet and handed it to her. 'My grandmother's favourite roses. I bought you some, to say thank you for helping me these past few days.'

'Oh.' The little spark that had lit up her eyes disappeared. He wasn't doing this right. He wasn't saying the right things. None of this was working out how he'd planned.

'They're beautiful. Thank you.' She was disappointed. She'd been hoping for something more. And so had he.

He moved forward, pulling her close, and whispered in her ear, 'Look closely, Carrie.'

She held up the bouquet to her nose and took a deep breath, savouring the smell of the roses. 'Where did you get them in the middle of this snow, Dan? They must have cost a fortune.' She still hadn't noticed. She still hadn't seen what he'd done.

He held up the bag he had in his other hand and pulled out a bundle—also tied with pink ribbon. She looked surprised and took the bundle from his hands. It was DVDs. *The Great Escape, Dirty Dancing, Finding Nemo, Toy Story* and a whole host of musicals. A little smile appeared on her face. 'What did you get these for, Dan?'

He gulped. He was going to have to spell it out. 'I figured if we were staying in a lot, we might need to expand our DVD collection. I thought we'd start with some favourites for us both.'

Her eyes finally caught sight of it. The key hanging from the pink ribbon on the bouquet. 'What's this for?'

'It's for you.'

'For me?' Her smile was starting to broaden and the sparkle to appear in her eyes again.

He caught a whiff of her scent. Freesias. More subtle than the roses. Sweeter. Something he could happily smell for the rest of his life. Who needed candles?

He pressed his hands firmly on her hips, pulling her closer to him. 'What's the point of having two apartments when we could easily have one?'

She wound her hands around his neck. 'One?'

He nodded and smiled. 'One.'

'What about the getting-to-know-you dates?'

'What about them?'

'Aren't we missing some stuff out here?'

'Honey, if you want to do some getting-to-know-you, then I'm your man.'

He bent to kiss her.

'You know, Dan, I think you could be right.'

'Carrie McKenzie, you're killing me. Will you look inside the roses, please?'

She wrinkled her nose and caught the glint of a diamond nestled inside one of the roses.

He sighed. 'Finally!'

He got down on one knee. 'Carrie McKenzie, I've never connected with anyone the way I've connected with you. I don't care where we stay, whether it's here or in London. All I know is I want us to be together. Carrie McKenzie, will you be my wife?'

He slid the ring onto her finger. She smiled. 'Aren't you supposed to wait for an answer?' She held up the ring, watching the perfect diamond glint in the sun.

He whispered in her ear, 'I'm not going to risk it. I'm hoping it's a yes.'

'Oh, it's definitely a yes,' she whispered as she wrapped her hands around his neck and started kissing him.

* * * * *

COMING NEXT MONTH FROM

HARLEQUIN

Romance

Available February 4, 2014

#4411 DARING TO TRUST THE BOSS
by Susan Meier
On a business trip to Italy, accountant-turned-PA Olivia Prentiss sees straight through her gorgeous boss's hard and proud exterior to a man hiding a far more vulnerable edge....

#4412 RESCUED BY THE MILLIONAIRE
by Cara Colter
When Trixie Marsh appeals for her neighbor Daniel Riverton's help with her nieces, he's in for big trouble! But it's not just the adorable twins who are melting his heart....

#4413 HEIRESS ON THE RUN
by Sophie Pembroke
When fate throws runaway heiress Lady Faith Fowlmere into the path of Lord Dominic Beresford, she realizes that this time, if she runs, she might just leave her heart behind....

#4414 THE SUMMER THEY NEVER FORGOT
by Kandy Shepherd
Everything has changed in the past twelve years, but Sandy Adams's heart still races at the sight of Ben Morgan, her first love. Would a trip down memory lane offer a second chance...for both of them?

HRLPCNM0114

LARGER-PRINT BOOKS!

GET 2 FREE LARGER-PRINT NOVELS PLUS

2 FREE GIFTS!

◆ HARLEQUIN®

Romance

From the Heart, For the Heart

YES! Please send me 2 FREE LARGER-PRINT Harlequin® Romance novels and my 2 FREE gifts (gifts are worth about $10). After receiving them, if I don't wish to receive any more books, I can return the shipping statement marked "cancel." If I don't cancel, I will receive 4 brand-new novels every month and be billed just $4.84 per book in the U.S. or $5.24 per book in Canada. That's a savings of at least 19% off the cover price! It's quite a bargain! Shipping and handling is just 50¢ per book in the U.S. and 75¢ per book in Canada.* I understand that accepting the 2 free books and gifts places me under no obligation to buy anything. I can always return a shipment and cancel at any time. Even if I never buy another book, the two free books and gifts are mine to keep forever.

119/319 HDN F43Y

Name	(PLEASE PRINT)	
Address		Apt. #
City	State/Prov.	Zip/Postal Code

Signature (if under 18, a parent or guardian must sign)

Mail to the Harlequin® Reader Service:
IN U.S.A.: P.O. Box 1867, Buffalo, NY 14240-1867
IN CANADA: P.O. Box 609, Fort Erie, Ontario L2A 5X3
Want to try two free books from another line?
Call 1-800-873-8635 or visit www.ReaderService.com.

* Terms and prices subject to change without notice. Prices do not include applicable taxes. Sales tax applicable in N.Y. Canadian residents will be charged applicable taxes. Offer not valid in Quebec. This offer is limited to one order per household. Not valid for current subscribers to Harlequin Romance Larger-Print books. All orders subject to credit approval. Credit or debit balances in a customer's account(s) may be offset by any other outstanding balance owed by or to the customer. Please allow 4 to 6 weeks for delivery. Offer available while quantities last.

Your Privacy—The Harlequin® Reader Service is committed to protecting your privacy. Our Privacy Policy is available online at www.ReaderService.com or upon request from the Harlequin Reader Service.

We make a portion of our mailing list available to reputable third parties that offer products we believe may interest you. If you prefer that we not exchange your name with third parties, or if you wish to clarify or modify your communication preferences, please visit us at www.ReaderService.com/consumerchoice or write to us at Harlequin Reader Service Preference Service, P.O. Box 9062, Buffalo, NY 14269. Include your complete name and address.

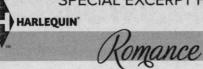
Here's a sneak peek at DARING TO TRUST THE BOSS
by Susan Meier

SOMEHOW THEY'D ENDED up standing face-to-face again. Under the luxurious blanket of stars, next to the twinkling blue water, the only sound the slight hum of the filter for the pool.

He reached out and cupped the side of her face.

"You are a brave, funny woman, Miss Prentiss."

Though she knew it was dangerous to get too personal with him, especially since his nearness already had her heart thrumming and her knees weak, she was only human. And even if it was a teeny tiny inconsequential thing, she didn't want to give up the one innocent pleasure she was allowed to get from him.

She caught his gaze. "Olivia."

"Excuse me?"

"I like it when you call me Olivia."

He took a step closer. "Really?"

She shrugged, trying to make light of her request. "Everybody calls me Vivi. Sometimes it makes me feel six again. Being called Olivia makes me feel like an adult."

"Or a woman."

The way he said *woman* sent heat rushing through her. Once again, he'd seen right through her ploy and might even realize she was attracted to him—

Oh, who was she kidding? He *knew* she was attracted to him.

But even as yearning nudged her to be bold, reality intruded. The guy she finally, finally wanted to trust was rich, sophisticated, so far out of her league she was lucky to be working for him. She knew better than to get romantically involved with someone like him.

She stepped back. "I wouldn't go that far."

He caught her hand and tugged her to him. "I would."

He kissed her so quickly that her knees nearly buckled and her brain reeled. She could have panicked. Could have told him to go slow because she hadn't done this in a while, or even stop because this was wrong. But nobody, no kiss, had ever made her feel the warm, wonderful, scary sensations saturating her entire being right now. Not just her body, but her soul.

His lips moved over hers smoothly, expertly, shooting fire and ice down her spine. Her breath froze in her chest. Then he opened his mouth over hers and her lips automatically parted.

The fire and ice shooting down her spine exploded in her middle, reminding her of where this would go if she didn't stop him. Now. She was so far out of Tucker's league, it was foolish to even consider kissing him.

She jerked away, stepped back. His glistening green eyes had narrowed with confusion. He didn't understand why she'd stopped him.

Longing warred with truth. If he could pretend their stations in life didn't matter, she could pretend. Couldn't she?

DARING TO TRUST THE BOSS
by Susan Meier
is available February 4, 2014,
wherever books and ebooks are sold!

HREXP0114